To all the girlies that want to go on an adventure without leaving their house.

CONTENTS

Prologue — 1

1. Marilyn — 3
2. Marilyn — 15
3. Lilith — 23
4. Marilyn — 33
5. Vale — 41
6. Nicodemus — 48
7. Marilyn — 58
8. Marilyn — 66
9. Zephyrus — 76
10. Zephyrus — 85
11. Marilyn — 96
12. Slade — 104
13. Marilyn — 113
14. Lilith — 119
15. Marilyn — 127
16. Marilyn — 134
17. Ares — 142
18. Zephyrus — 149
19. Slade — 156
20. Nicodemus — 162
21. Ares — 169
22. Vale — 174
23. Marilyn — 181
24. Marilyn — 191
25. Lilith — 198
26. Marilyn — 207
27. Nicodemus — 212
28. Marilyn — 219

29. Vale — 226

30. Marilyn — 234

Thank you for reading! — 243
Have you left a review? — 245

PROLOGUE

The Devil doesn't come dressed in a red cape and pointy horns; he comes as everything you've ever wished for.

MARILYN

PRESENT DAY

When you imagine hell, you imagine that it's probably going to be hot. Unlike a vacation, you probably aren't going to have a good time. How do you have a good time when little men are running around with pitchforks trying to skewer you like a witchy kabob?

Despite considering this place hell for the last six months, Blackwood Academy doesn't look anything like what I imagined. Would you believe that the sun shines over Blackwood the same way it shines over Hawthorne or Ridgeview? Imagine my surprise when we drove up to the gates and a swirling cloud of doom didn't suddenly appear above the academy.

"This is it?" I ask my parents as I unload my bags from the back. Four oversize suitcases contain all of my worldly possessions, or at least the ones I was allowed to bring with me. "Where are the buildings with a thousand years of grime and decay?" The academy looks like a God damn Ivy League university with its large, sprawling campus full of ivory buildings. The most nefarious thing in sight are the vines climbing up the sides of the building. Real spooky shit, if you ask me. "Where's the portal to hell?"

Mercer gives me a generous smile that says he can't wait until I'm gone and everything goes back to the way it should have been. He attended Hawthorne Academy with my mother, Jacqueline, and both of them feel uncomfortable with the idea that their daughter is attending a school for the wicked. "You're being very dramatic today, Marilyn. This academy is no different than the others." Says the man who was so upset that The Council placed me here that he stormed out of the house and returned three days later smelling like a distillery.

"Come on," I shoot him a teasing look. "You can't honestly tell me that Blackwood is what you wanted for me." I'm poking a bear. An out-of-shape, alcoholic bear, but a bear nonetheless.

Jacqueline climbs out of the car with a look on her face that says the academy isn't much to look at. Her nose crinkles in disgust and she has to tear her eyes away from the buildings to keep from tearing up with grief. Even though the lawn is perfectly manicured and the vibe of Blackwood Academy isn't far off from what she told me Hawthorne was like, it's clear that Jacqueline Snow thinks this place is beneath her. "Marilyn," her tone is condescending, "this place is *nice*. It's very cute. I hope you enjoy yourself. Mercer, we should get going. I have a benefit next weekend and I need to get back to Earth." God bless my mother. Or strike her dead. Both are good options.

Neither of my parents ever wanted kids. When they had me, it was by accident; subtle proof that their magic wasn't completely infallible. Birth control pills and spells only conjured up a baby, the exact opposite of their intended purpose.

My father walks around the car and eyes my luggage. For a second, I think he contemplates offering to help me carry it inside. But then the look in his eyes disappears and his gaze turns to Jacqueline. "Remember your first day at Hawthorne?" He asks her in an uncharacteristically intimate tone.

Jacqueline ignores him for a moment, but when he reaches out to grab her hand and bring it to his lips, a half smile appears on hers. "You were a cad, Mercer Bayard, and I'll tell anyone who listens that I was a fool to accept that first date."

It's like watching a twisted Gomez and Morticia as Mercer pulls Jacqueline into him. She's tall and lithe, willowy like the models she hires to wear her clothes. He's a couple of inches shorter than her and he's packed on the pounds over his last few years of binge drinking himself to sleep every night. "I might have dated a lot of women, but I only had eyes for you, darling."

I might look up to them as an idealistic couple if it wasn't for the fact that I haven't seen them touch one another in a decade.

My father spends all his time going over cases. He's an attorney in Meira'mor specializing in Improper Magical Usage. While he often defends minors who can't keep their magic from spilling out of them, his bread and butter are criminals that break the law and need someone to get them out of trouble. When he isn't knee-deep in paperwork and magical law, he's several glasses deep into a bottle of bourbon.

My mother is never home. She didn't quite *find herself* in Meira'mor after I was born. She spends most of her time on Earth running a fashion empire and making art. Whenever she deigns to come back to this side of the portal, it's at a strange hour of the day when nobody is awake, least of all my drunkard of a father. While he's passed out on the couch or in his study, she's making gourmet meals for herself at the crack of dawn before falling into a twelve-hour slumber.

"Alright. This was fun." I announce over the two of them canoodling against the car. Maybe now that I'm leaving the house, they'll rekindle their relationship. I know that I'm the reason they can't bear to look at or touch one another, but if I'm gone, maybe their contempt for each other will be gone as well. "If I get killed here, do you want the Headmaster to call you first or just send you my remains?"

Jacqueline tears her eyes away from my father only to roll them at me. "Don't be ridiculous, Marilyn. This place is perfect for you. You won't be *killed* or anything else." She says the word 'killed' the same way she would talk about bodily fluids at the dining table, with disgust.

When The Council told my parents that my soul and powers were drawn toward darkness and thus suited for Blackwood, they demanded an appeal. As good, hardworking, and ambitious role models, I was brought up to be a legacy of Hawthorne Academy. The Council performed an appeal at their behest, but my results didn't change. '*Your daughter has a dark heart,*' they told my parents. '*She will do things that will test the boundaries of magic and morality.*'

"Oh, so it's perfect for me now but it wasn't six months ago when The Coun—" Jacqueline cuts me off with a glare.

"It has taken me all this time to get used to what you are, *Marilyn,*" she spits out my name like she's tasting bad sushi, "can't you just say goodbye and go? You're ruining this for me." With a huff of frustration, my mother averts her eyes as if she can't bear to look at me anymore. "I thought this would be a special day for us. Your father and I were going to show you around Hawthorne and introduce you to all the secret locations that only veterans of the school know about. But instead, we're standing in front of an academy with the *foulest* reputation and you're being a brat. Can't you respect me for once and just leave when you know I'm uncomfortable?" To say I have mommy issues would be an understatement. I have daddy issues as well, but that's a can of worms to open on another day.

I clench my left hand, feeling the presence of my ring against the middle and pinky fingers as I tighten my fist. The bags beside me hover off the ground in response. "Goodbye, mother." The words sound tense as they're whistled between my teeth. I walk away, leaving behind me a pair of whispering parents that never wanted a child. Whatever they're saying will be forgotten when they leave the campus, only to resurface on holidays and summer break.

I make my way across the lawn and read the names of the buildings carved in ivory stone. Forge Hall. There's where we dine, I remember it from the campus brochure. Latham Hall. Where all of our classes take place. There is a greenhouse that takes up a large chunk of land. In the sprawling space around it, there are gardens heading in every direction. The Klein Observatory. The Warnack Library. Crowne Chapel. Buckley Hall. And finally, McCabe Village. Where the students reside. A few more buildings shoot off in other directions, but this is my first stop.

McCabe Village is a structure of three buildings narrowly connected by a hallway with full-length windows running the entire fifty yards. When I read the history of the campus, it was said that the student living area was designed to focus on inclusivity. We might all be outcasts in society's eyes, but we were outcasts together.

I enter McCabe's first building and I'm inundated with dark wood and hard floors. Everything feels formal and cold, even the fireplace burning in building A's common room. I pass by a group of students who give me a sneer just for looking at them. I half consider turning around and asking what their problem is, but I keep walking instead.

My room number is easy to remember. 111. The first number indicates the floor, the second two digits indicate the room. Despite McCabe being five stories tall, I've been given a view of the ground floor.

Hallways shoot out in various directions. In silver script on the wall, numbers tell you where you're at. 110–113 is where I turn. At the end of my hallway is a floor-to-ceiling window that illuminates the space. In the eventuality that the sun has gone down and you've left your room, there are lights on the walls to brighten the path. It feels a little claustrophobic as I make my way to the end, but somehow, it's still more comforting than being at home. Between 110 and 111, and 112 and 113, are bathroom doors. One for every two rooms to accommodate four people.

The door to room 111 is open. The expansive space has two full-size beds, two desks, two closets, and a decent-sized living space in the center for a couch, two chairs, and a small coffee table. The furniture almost sections off the two halves of the room, creating a barrier between my half and my roommate's.

Speaking of my roommate, she's already here. She sits in the center of our room sprawled out on the couch with her feet thrown over the edge. I can tell from this angle that she's tall and lithe, just like my mother. "Oh, god, you reek," she announces with a sneer. "What is that smell?" And just as bitchy.

I raise an eyebrow as I step inside. I don't smell anything particularly heinous, but what do I know? Maybe her magic manifests as super smell, though how that would get her placed in Blackwood is beyond me. "Hello to you, too."

She throws her feet toward the floor and rights herself. Her sparkling, gold eyes look me up and down as she takes me in. "What's your race?"

The hair on my arms bristles like I'm under attack. The Council warned me about this. Blackwood Academy is full of demons, shifters, werewolves, and other dangerous creatures. *'They won't take too kindly to a witch. They view your kind as less powerful than theirs.'*

"Hello?" The woman stands up and waves her hand in my direction. "Can you hear me or are you just stupid?"

Now that I think about it, I probably could have saved on tuition and stayed home if I had known my roommate was going to be just like my mom. "My *name* is Marilyn." With her things stacked in front of the bed on the far right, I walk over to the left. My designated space, complete with bedding and a neatly folded duvet cover.

"My name is Lilith and I'm a *shifter*. Your turn, princess. I'm waiting." To drive her point home, Lilith starts tapping her shoe against the marble floor.

I let my things descend to the floor and turn to face my new roommate for the next five years. Her hair is purple, almost iridescent. With every move she makes, it looks like it changes shades. Her glittering gold eyes are flecked with black in the iris. She's a dragon shifter.

I have one of two options. I could lie about my race. Eventually, the truth will come out and Lilith will probably be pissed. So I stick with facing her anger upfront. "I'm a witch and a wearer." I hold up my left hand where my silver ring lies.

Lilith snorts in the most unladylike fashion. "Jesus fucking Christ," she swears. "I could have had anyone in the school. I could have been paired with another fucking shifter, for Christ's sake. And they gave me the fucking dud? How are you supposed to protect me in a fight?"

"I didn't realize we were getting in a fight anytime soon," I deadpan.

She walks across the room toward me. As she gets closer, her height becomes more clear. I'm only 5'3", but standing in front of me, she has to be half a foot taller, maybe more. My mother would die to have Lilith wearing her designs. She has good bone structure and the way she moves draws your eye to her. "I knew you smelled different, but I didn't know it was because you were one of *them*. How did you get in here?"

The condescending tone is so reminiscent of Jacqueline that it ignites something inside of me. "Through the front door. What about you?"

A smile pulls at the corners of her lips as she stares down at me. "You're kind of funny, witch."

"I prefer Marilyn." I stand my ground because it's day one. If I fold now, I run the risk of being a nobody and a nothing for the next five years. And maybe I still will be a nobody and a nothing when it's all said and done, but not because of Lilith.

She leans forward and inhales deeply, breathing me in. "And I prefer strength in numbers. What's a pipsqueak like *you* gonna do for *me*?"

Blackwood Academy will teach me how to harness my powers. They'll open up my abilities from their core and help me to grow into my strength. But right now, I use what I have to drive Lilith's luggage across the room until it crashes into her legs. She falls backward, landing hard on her tailbone. "Fuck with me and find out, *princess*," I return her condescending term of endearment from earlier.

Her eyes flare dark, the gold turning to an onyx black. For a second I think that I need to brace myself for a shift. But then, she starts laughing. Lilith sticks her hand in my direction, demanding that I help her to her feet. "You're a spunky little thing. Maybe you'll be able to fight after all. And if not," she adds, "at least you can make me laugh."

What's with all this talk of fighting? How did I get roped into magical fight club and how do I get out?

As if reading my mind, Lilith releases my hand and takes a step back, shoving her luggage away with a kick. "They don't tell you about the Warrior Center in the brochures. You have to be a legacy to find out about that. The Headmaster likes to watch us compete, generally pitting room versus room to see what kind of pairs perform the best."

"That's sick," I say, paling in response.

Lilith turns her back on me and walks to the couch. "No, that's Blackwood Academy. We're the worst of the worst here." She throws herself back down and kicks her feet up on the coffee table this time. "If they don't find out what we can do, how will they know what to protect Meira'mor from?"

I can manipulate matter. My magic is harnessed through a ring made by ancient men and women with power that I could only dream of. At any moment, all they have to do is remove the strongest source of my power and I'm useless; the universe doesn't need protecting from me. "I'm sorry to be such a disappointment."

Lilith looks me up and down with a critical gaze. She looks at me as if she's staring into the depths of my soul. "You won't be," she decides after a moment. "If anyone scares the shit out of the scientists and sadists in the Warrior Center, it's going to be you. Do you know the last time a witch was sent to Blackwood?"

"1942," I respond. I looked it up when The Council said that this would be my home for the next five years.

"You're a rare breed around these halls, princess. That means that somewhere beyond that quiet exterior and seething rage is a monster." Her lips curl into a devious grin. "And I can fuck shit up with a monster by my side."

The difference between Meira'mor and Earth isn't magic. The difference between Meira'mor and Earth is music. And the drinking age.

Who decided that twenty-year-olds couldn't drink in this universe? I'm in desperate need of a whiskey coke if I'm going to make it to midnight. The bars in this God-forsaken place stay open until 2:00 am. What person in their right mind stays up that late? Is that why we're always warned about drugs when we cross the portal from Meira'mor to Earth? Is this species surviving on a little white helper taken directly up the nostril?

I feel old, or maybe just wise beyond my years. Twenty-year-old humans still have a lot of learning to do; twenty-year-old witches might as well be considered middle-aged. We still need to attend an academy, but it's to harness and strengthen our powers, not learn how to do our taxes.

Frankly, I hate coming to Earth. The guards take my ring at the portal and I'm left with little more magic than a street magician. My powers are weakened here for the sake of the humans. It makes me feel vulnerable. And naked.

I rub the ring finger on my left hand absent-mindedly as I look around Mahogany, a packed club with blaring music. There's a man trying to catch my eye, but I stare right through him. Off in the distance is the bar, the bane of my existence. They won't let me buy anything on this damn planet. It's as if capitalism doesn't start until you're twenty-one.

Earlier, I had to pay some creep at a gas station to buy me a pack of cigarettes. He offered to do it for free as long as I showed him my tits, but my self-esteem wasn't that low. Not to mention this dress is too tight to be pulling out my breasts for a stranger on the street. I had to pay the low, low fee of $10 to get him to even consider buying cigarettes for someone underage and another $10 to get him to go inside and fetch me the product.

Cigarettes are a nasty habit. I always wake up the morning after a trip to Earth smelling the remnants of alcohol sweating through my pores and cheap nicotine engrained in the fibers of my clothes. But nothing goes with a drink and talking to a human quite like a cigarette. I could use one now to tame my nerves, but instead, I focus on charming a man into buying me alcohol first.

I feel my victim's presence just a moment before his hands grab my hips from behind. Over the loud music bumping from the speakers, he yells in my ear, "Can I get you something, gorgeous?"

I smell tequila on his breath. For a moment, I close my eyes and bask in the scent of the liquor. "Whiskey coke," I order. I don't know who he is and I don't care. If he gets me a drink, maybe I'll let him have a dance or two. I'm generous to people who are generous to me.

His hands slide off my hips and I no longer feel his presence nearby. With my drink coming soon, I can start to relax. I take a deep breath and let the beat pour through my veins. My body aches to move, so I shift from foot to foot as I grow accustomed to the rhythm.

A gaggle of women at the bar stare at me with mixed emotions on their faces. One looks ready to scratch my eyes out. Another looks on wistfully. They hate me. They want to be me. C'est la vie.

I wish I had friends in this universe. I've taken a few lovers, but we never spoke after the night we spent together. I come to bars and clubs like Mahogany searching for a good time, not a long time. If I wanted friends, I'd stay in Meira'mor. Though I guess I have to make new friends now. Cassandra is headed to Maplecroft, Samara started at Hawthorne last year, and Faith begins at Silverleaf in the spring. They're not going where I am and that'll make maintaining our friendship over the next five years a little difficult.

But to be quite honest, I'm as envious of the women at the bar as they are of me. I didn't come to Mahogany tonight with my best girlfriends, all of us hoping to find a man who might be the one. I came here with the intention of hooking up with a human one last time before I start school in a few weeks. After my term at Blackwood begins, I don't know when I'll have the chance to return. I don't even know if I'll want to. I came to get my kicks in one last time before the professors and students of my new home change me forever.

"Hey, beautiful." Another man approaches and his energy feels strangely bereft, tickling the dark parts of my soul as he draws nearer. "Can I have this dance?" He speaks melodically and carries no drinks. His eyes are hidden behind a sheath of bangs that undoubtedly obscure his vision, but he looks harmless enough.

I let him take my hand and lead me into the fray. He isn't the one for me tonight, but I don't mind giving up a few minutes of my time. And when he places his hands on the curve of my hip, he is as gentle as he is quiet. He moves me across the floor in quick, two-step beats, never saying another word. I catch a glimpse of his eyes as our movement draws the bangs away from his face, but he turns his head before I can memorize any identifying features.

The man who said he'd get me a drink returns as the music changes. "Hey," he butts in with a glare, "I thought you and I were together."

Side-Swept Bangs releases his grip on my waist and takes a step backward as if he's some gallant knight stepping aside for the king. "Sorry," he apologizes quickly. "I didn't know this was your girl," he swears. "All we did was dance."

I don't owe anyone any apologies. I didn't come here with anyone and I damn sure won't be leaving with either of these two men. "Is that my drink?" I take a step toward the proffered beverage and feel my soul teem with excitement at the prospect.

"You think I'm gonna get a drink for a girl who won't even wait for me to come back?" His energy is off; I can feel it in the vibrations coming off of him in waves. I should walk away from this situation before it gets out of control. But I've never really been known for doing what I'm supposed to.

I step forward and place my fingers around the glass, enveloping his hand in mine. "Just give me the drink, dude. It's not that big of a deal." The sharp edge of my tone sets him off. Side-Swept Bangs walks away, disappearing into the crowd as if he never existed.

The atmosphere shifts as the stranger rips the

glass out of my hand. I barely register what's happening when he baptizes me in whiskey and coke. "It's not that big of a deal," he sneers, repeating my words back at me as I stand there drenched in liquor and sticky sweet soda.

This is why there are guards at the portal. I'm a Wearer, meaning that my magic is tied to a blessed item that harnesses my power. When you're studying at the academy or when you're underage, the guards are there to ensure you don't explode on the humans or do something that would jeopardize Meira'mor. For me, that meant taking away my ring.

In retrospect, it was a good idea. If I was wearing it now, I could take the glass from his hand and smash it over his head without moving a muscle. Or I could grab one of those barstools and drive it into his back. Or I could take the baton out of the security guard's belt and beat him to death with it.

Upon introspection, I can understand why I'm being sent to Blackwood. Some people would take a drink to the face with grace and dignity. Faith would apologize for her behavior and ask if she could get the person a replacement. Samara would fume about it for the rest of the night, but she'd never act on her anger. Cassandra would walk away from the situation and go home. I'm the only one of us that considers killing a man over it. Maybe I should get help.

"Apologize to the lady." The voice that cuts into

our conversation is deep; it booms over the speakers. I shift my head to the left to see a hulk of a man walking up, my veritable knight-in-shining-armor.

The man with the glass wavers as he looks at the intruder. I see his eyes trail upward to meet my knight's gaze. His mouth opens as if he's about to say something, but instead, he drops the glass and darts into the crowd, leaving us with an explosion of shards.

The beast of a man turns to look at me and I find myself getting lost in his eyes. They're the color of acid-washed dark denim, or perhaps the sea at night. The hues are swirled together—the dark blue of the ocean and the foam from the waves. I've never seen eyes like this before. "Let's get you cleaned up," he says in a way that sounds more like a come-on than a statement of fact.

He reaches out for me, hand grabbing mine and pulling me through the crowd. My senses are overwhelmed and I can't explain why. "Let's go outside!" I yell as we get closer to the bathroom.

I don't want to be trapped in a close space with him. Between his broad shoulders and sharply defined features, I'm afraid that the fluorescent lights in the bathroom will reveal that he isn't as good-looking as he appears in the dimly lit club. Or worse, that he is.

Without skipping a beat, my hulking knight walks past the restrooms and escorts me to an emergency exit. A sign says that an alarm will sound if the door is opened, but the beast doesn't stop. He pushes through the metal door and leads me into the alley. No alarm sounds, no one knows that we're out here. The music in the club muffles as the door slams shut behind us.

"You want a cigarette?" He reaches into his back pocket and pulls out a pack.

I summon a lighter from my purse. "You want a light?"

He's the one. He's the man I'm taking home tonight.

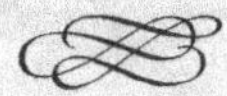

"My mother is a professor. She's not one of the scientists in the Warrior Center, but she's big on experimentation." My new roommate reminds me of a porcelain doll; if I drop her too hard, she might break. Telling her that my mother was brought in to teach at Blackwood because her experimentations involved cutting people open and using their body parts and fluids to enhance other races seems like one of the things that might break her.

I don't mind Marilyn though. Even my keen sense of smell that picks up the scent of burning fire whenever she's around doesn't bother me all that much. She's small and funny, pretty in a delicate sort of way. I can see myself coming around to liking her.

"I was accepted into Blackwood before The

Council even sent me here," I boast. "Being born a dragon shifter practically ensures your placement."

Marilyn nods her head in quiet agreement, stifling a yawn as we pass by the library. "My parents thought that was the case for me and Hawthorne Academy," she says after a few moments.

My nose wrinkles automatically. Not only can I *not* imagine being anywhere else, but I also can't see myself ever attending Hawthorne. Not even if The Council sent me there. "The school for the ambitious and determined? Believe me, you're better off here." At the school for the wicked and depraved.

She pushes a strand of hair behind her ear and nods her head in faux agreement. "You mean at the school where they pit us against one another in underground battle matches? That's where I belong?"

A self-hating Blackwood student, they're a rarity around these parts. Most of the men and women that walk through the gates of the campus know that deep down they're as sick and twisted as the school's reputation. "Don't knock what you are, Marilyn," I chide. "This school has a history of producing some of the most powerful beings to ever exist."

"This school has a history of raising villains. You know the kind, they terrorize our world or the humans until it gets to the point that someone has to take them out." Marilyn snaps at me. "I might not have belonged at Hawthorne Academy, but I can tell you that no one has left their hallowed halls, started a war, and faced decades of prison time for war crimes against their home universe."

I wonder if she's met my dad. Talk about a guy who made being a villain his entire personality trait. "Po-tay-to, po-tah-to," I respond with a shrug. "So what if people have taken the things they've learned here and used them for evil? It's no different than someone leaving Silverleaf and deciding to go genocidal on the fae race."

Maybe it's a little different, but not enough to tip the scales. To me, it sounds like the nature versus nurture debate. Sending someone to Blackwood doesn't mean they'll wind up evil. Teaching them how to harness their powers doesn't mean they'll wind up evil. The only thing that can determine a person's potential for wicked behavior is the person themselves.

We carry on across the campus, each step bringing us closer to Forge Hall. On introduction day, the Blackwood Academy staff hosts a banquet for its students. The older students are given places of honor around the hall. Those in their fifth and final year are placed at an elevated table where everyone in the room can see and look up at them. New students, like Marilyn and myself, sit in the back and listen to Headmaster Merryweather drone on about the rules and regulations.

"The campus is beautiful," Marilyn wisely decides to change the subject. "I was expecting dark brick and dead grass. This is a pleasant surprise."

Witches. They're raised so differently than the rest of us. "Blackwood isn't too bad. I've been coming here pretty much my whole life. My dad used to be a professor as well, but then he kind of went mad and had to be institutionalized." My mom was the one who had him locked up. There wasn't anything particularly wrong with him, but I suspect that he was a covert experiment of mom's. She probably injected a little too much werewolf blood into his cocktails each night just to see what would happen. "But besides that, it's a pretty decent place. The food is good. The professors really know their shit. In terms of education, it's one of the best you're going to get in Meira'mor. We're a very well-rounded academy for the reputation that we have."

I see Marilyn catch a few glances as we walk across the campus. Eyes and nostrils flare as people start to realize what she is, whether by smell or other magical methods. They treat her like she's a carnival sideshow or a car wreck; they can't look away. "Everybody here seems real welcoming," she mumbles as she registers what's happening. Marilyn faces forward, training her eyes to only look ahead. I admire her strength, that's for sure.

"Listen," I reach across the small expanse

between us and brush her forearm with my finger-tips to get her attention, "you're not like the rest of us. You carry yourself differently. You look different. You smell different. Hell, you even act different. You've got to give people a chance to get used to it." I didn't meet my first witch until I was twelve years old. My mom maintains that several of the people we've met at stores or in restaurants were witches, but I doubt her claims. Many of the people at Black-wood probably have the same history with witches that I do.

But Marilyn didn't have the same upbringing, as evidenced by her soliloquy on respecting all races big and small. "I wasn't taught to look down on shifters or vampires or demons or anyone else. We were warned about wizards," she adds, "but that was more along the lines of men usurping women's powers and the law being unable to do anything about it."

That sounds crazy to me. The magic that I was born with, the abilities that I have, can't be taken from me. The fact that I can cut off Marilyn's ring finger or slip that silver band off and watch her strength decrease is incredulous. I'd rather die than be a witch. "They'll come around," I tell her after a moment, shrugging my shoulders. There isn't much else I can do to reassure her that eventually, one day, these people will be okay with the fact that she's different. "Be grateful you're a witch and not a succubus. I'd have burned you alive if you were a succubus," I joke. Except it isn't really a joke.

Out of the corner of my eye, I can see Marilyn's jaw drop as she picks up a mask of confusion. "What?" She asks, exasperated. "What's wrong with succubi?"

Thinking about it sends a shiver down my spine. "Maybe it's a Blackwood thing." I'm not racist by any means; I just have strong opinions about people who live up to the stereotype of their race. I try to explain it to her. "A group of succubi shows up every year and they're always inducted into the Succubus Squad. Think of a clique of mean girls. They walk from hall to hall looking for people to pick on, hoist in the air, melt with their eyes. Whatever. They're pretty much the shittiest people in existence, at least while they're at the academy." Outside these halls? Who knows. I've never seen one on the streets.

"Speaking of shitty people you should stay away from, consider keeping your distance from the Blackwood Five." Nicodemus' blonde hair and insufferable laugh catch my eye from across the courtyard.

Marilyn's face twists and contorts. Her eyes narrow as she stares ahead at the group of boys I'm gesturing to. "I'm sorry. The who?" But she never stops staring at the group of boys dead ahead. There is recognition in her gaze.

"The Blackwood Five," I repeat. "That's four of them over there." I nod in their direction. From the angle of Marilyn's head, I can tell she's already looking at them. "They may be attractive, but they'll ruin your life." As if sensing us talking about them, I see eyes start to turn in our direction. "The Blackwood Five are a pack of demons. Sometimes people call them the horde."

My roommate's walk slows to a crawl. "Lilith," she mumbles under her breath.

But she speaks so low that I don't hear her. "That's Vale. Everybody calls him The Beast because he's so big." Talk about a man who spends more time at the gym than reading a textbook. "He's the self-appointed leader of the Blackwood Five and the biggest dick on campus. Mind you, I don't *just* mean his personality." I shudder just thinking about it. Last year he tossed a first year off campus. He used his abilities to physically lift the kid into the air and chuck him over the gate. "He's easily packing 9" of thick, veiny, demonic dick beneath his slacks. Not that I know personally," I add, "but he's shown half the school so it's pretty much common knowledge at this point."

Marilyn raises her voice a little louder. "Lilith," she calls my name.

This time, I hear her, but I think she's about to tell me that Vale is attractive and I won't stand for that. Not when I know what he's capable of. "There's Nicodemus. He's the pretty boy of the group and sweet enough to break your teeth on." His family came to my house for dinner once and I think by the end of it, I got a cavity from thinking about how sweet he was. "He's pretty fucked up beneath the surface tough. He's got the gift of biochemical manipulation and I've seen him use it to fuck up the molecular structure of someone's genetics before."

I direct my eyes to the twins. They're laughing as if all is well in the world, but I know what lies under those smiles. "Ares is the sexy half of the Bloodstone twins. And by sexy, I just mean he isn't a complete asshole. I heard he's a shadow walker. I've never met one personally, but it sounds like a cool party trick." With a dip of my head in the opposite direction, I introduce her to the other twin. "That's Slade the Sadist. He's a Dream Bender. Sometimes twins get the same power, but the two of them didn't I guess. As far as I know, Ares doesn't use his abilities to fuck with people on a daily basis. Slade, on the other hand, takes great pleasure in digging through your nightmares and making them a reality." He could manifest people's good dreams if he wanted to, but that's not Slade's style.

Marilyn stops walking and grabs my arm, halting me in place as well. "You said the Blackwood *Five*. Where's the fifth one?"

"Oh, yeah, Zephyrus. I guess we're supposed to call him Professor Storm. He teaches a specialized course in alchemy with an emphasis on chaos and destruction. I've also heard he's gifted with pyrotechnic sorcery, but I've never seen it firsthand. He graduated two or three years ago at the top of his class. In fact, my mom talked about him a lot. She said she'd never seen a more gifted student." She doesn't consider me gifted, but you can't win them all. When you're a dragon with omnicompetence, there isn't much to be impressed by. So I can handle any situation, problem, or conflict. What's the big whoop?

I go on, finishing up telling Marilyn about Zephyrus. "The Headmaster has been trying to get him to teach here since the day he graduated. He's good with the students and a phenomenal kisser, according to my sister. She graduated last year and said that she made out with him by the lake once. I bet she did more than that, but she'd never admit it to me."

Once there's a lull in the conversation, Marilyn tightens her grip on my arm and pulls me closer to her. If she could stand on her toes to whisper in my ear, I bet she would. "We have a problem."

Right then, Ares turns around and catches the two of us in his purview. I see the smile on his face slide off as he looks at Marilyn. "Uh, what problem? If you're into any of those men," I start.

Marilyn groans and releases me. Ares elbows his brother and I see his lips move as he talks to the other two guys. All four pairs of eyes stare in our direction.

"I'm not *into* them, Lilith, but they *were* into me. Three or four weeks ago, actually."

"Did," I pause and try to gather my thoughts. Mom is always saying that I need to think before I speak. She always tells me that just because I know everything doesn't mean I should blurt out what I'm thinking. "Did you *fuck* the Blackwood Five?"

The demon foursome starts walking our way with Vale at the head of the pack. He clenches his fists repeatedly at his sides and his pretty blue eyes start flashing a demonic red.

"I was on Earth," Marilyn mumbles, "I didn't know who they were."

I look over at her. My tiny little roommate with her bright silver gaze and blushing cheeks looks like a different person now. Goodbye, porcelain doll I once imagined her to be five minutes ago. Hello, bad bitch who's going to get us both killed. "Remind me to kick your ass later."

I've heard dozens of stories from my mom about the Blackwood Five. They go around campus causing mischief and mayhem. They're the poster children for what Marilyn was afraid this academy would turn her into. And she had sex with them?

I try not to sleep with people that I hate, but witches really are built differently than the rest of us.

MARILYN

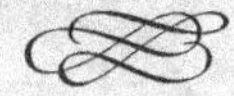

3 WEEKS BEFORE

"You got a name?" The beast of a man asks after taking a drag from the cigarette. He blows smoke from his lips and it smells like heaven.

God, I forgot how much I loved this universe on a Friday night. The men. The alcohol. The nightlife. It's unlike anything we have in Meira'mor.

I take a second to light my cigarette and bask in the ambiance before responding. "My friends call me Marilyn, but you can call me yours for the night if you'd like." I am brazen. I am bold. I've never been like this with a man before, but I kind of love it.

The alley that we're standing in is dark, lit only by a street light 100 yards away. There's a small floodlight above the emergency exit we just walked through, but the bulb needs to be replaced. The light flickers every few moments, threatening to shut off at any second. Dumpsters line the back of the businesses from here to the street. The faint smell of rotting food and trash is masked by a cool breeze.

Fucking in an alley in the middle of the night has never been on my bucket list. There's something about a proper bed, a bathroom, or even a place where the walls aren't coated in grime that has often held more appeal for me than a strip of concrete between two buildings. But the stranger's eyes smolder with lust as he looks at me, dampening my panties. If he wants to take me here and now, who am I to stop him?

"For the night?" He raises an eyebrow and looks me up and down. A tingling sensation races down my spine as he undresses me with his eyes. "What about for a quick fuck? I've got a busy schedule, Marilyn."

He strikes me as the asshole type. The kind of guy that if he ran into me on the streets, he'd expect *me* to apologize to *him*. Usually, I don't waste time on men like that, but something about the way he carries himself calls to my inner animal. She gnashes at the cage she's being held in, desperate to be free. She wants to be let loose on this man, to rake her fingers across his skin and scream that she hates him when she's coming all over his cock.

I take a glance at my watch, feigning boredom,

before looking at him again. I bet a man with broad shoulders like that could pick me up and bounce me on his dick without the aid of a wall to lean on. "Don't take too long, stud," I blow out a ring of smoke, "I've got places to be, too."

The right side of his mouth curls upward into a devious smirk. My knight-in-shining-armor takes one last, long drag of his cigarette before flicking it to the ground. He steps forward until his hulking figure is pressed against mine. The beast towers over me by a foot, looking down at me with a smoldering gaze that makes me clench my center in anticipation. "Drop the cigarette, honey," he breaks the silence, "the only thing you need to hold onto is me."

I have more for later if I need them. I let my borrowed stick fall to the ground and before I can even open my mouth to ask him what's next, he's hoisting me up and slamming me into the wall of the building. The gesture takes my breath away, literally. It catches me off guard and the pain steals my oxygen.

"Pull your panties to the side," he commands, his tone leaving no chance for me to broker an argument.

As I reach between us, I let my fingers slide down his chest. A black shirt clings to muscles that I would rather get on my knees and lick than simply caress. My dress has been helpfully pulled upward by the position I find myself in, bunching at my waist. The space between my thighs is hot with desire as I grab the side of my panties and unveil what's beneath.

"Now take out my cock." Once again, he tells me what to do. I reach forward to unbutton his jeans and reach inside. I'm met with a monster. His cock is so large that it takes both of my hands to unsheath it. I tear my eyes off him and meet his member face-to-face. "That's not going to fit," I announce.

He tightens his grip on my ass, fingers digging into my skin so hard that I swear he's going to leave bruises. "Make. It. Fit." He commands.

A shiver runs down my spine and it feels like my body follows his directions without any input from me. I guide his member to my slick entrance and pray that he doesn't rip me in two.

The second his head rubs against my arousal, he splits me open. I wrap my arms around his neck for a better grip and grit my teeth as he forces his way inside. "You know the best part of having a big dick?" His question is part whisper, part growl.

"No," I groan as he fills me up. "What's the best part?"

His head hits my cervix before he's all the way in. A jolt of pain rocks through my core, but it's quickly replaced with pleasure as he starts to thrust his hips back and forth. "Every pussy feels like a vice grip tightening around me." His lips come to my ear and I feel his warm breath tickle my lobe. "Especially yours. Your tight little cunt is suffocating. You feel like a sweater three sizes too small. And if you tighten your fucking kegel muscles one more time, I'm going to explode inside of you."

I throw my head back. Something about his dirty mouth sets me off. I wrap my legs around his waist and cross them at the ankle. He tries to pull out of me, but I pull him back in. "I want you to fucking tear me apart," I moan. "Fuck me until it hurts." He brings out the filthy side of me. Or maybe it's the alley. I don't know which is dirtier.

"You like this monster dick inside of you, don't you," he growls in my ear. Every word is punctuated with a thrust. My core expands to take all of him and he no longer slams into my cervix with each onslaught of his member. "You want me to fill your filthy little pussy full of my cum, don't you."

I've never liked dirty talk before. The men who were interested in it always seemed to take it too far, but every word this stranger says speaks to that beast inside of me that wants to be let out. "I want to milk your cock. I want to feel you dripping down my thighs when I go back inside."

He keeps going harder. The tip of his dick grazes my G-spot with every undulation and I'm slammed back into the wall over and over again as he fucks me. I can't tell what makes me short of breath: the pleasure or the pain. Both are exquisite.

"That's right. Take all of me until I tear you in two. Imagine me penetrating your ass right now." As if knowing that I need more stimulation, I feel his finger wiggle beneath my panties and find my forbidden flower. He presses his middle finger against the ring until it pops inside. "Just think about how you'd feel with this big, swollen cock right here."

I black out, or maybe I lose enough oxygen from screaming with pleasure that I forget a few moments. But when I '*wake*' back up, I'm coming on his cock. His finger is sliding in and out of my ass at the same pace as his member. I am flush all over. Despite the cool breeze in the alley, I am feverish.

My heart almost stops when he pulls his finger out of my ass and grabs tightly onto my thigh. He roars like an animal as he orgasms and not a drop of his juices are left when I'm through with him. I use my kegels to massage his member, doing exactly what I said I would. I milk him like a fucking cow until I'm so full of sperm that it's going to explode out of me when he pulls out.

"Fuck," he swears with an angry growl, "you're a fucking treat."

Navigating out of this position is harder than getting into it. The stranger pulls his dick out of me and even post-orgasm, he's a big boy. He's the kind of guy who can grow and show, if you know what I mean. Then he sets me on my feet and takes a few steps back to right himself.

I wiggle the fabric of my dress back down around my hips, replacing my panties over my cum-filled center. I'm a hostess Twinkie; all the cream is on the inside.

"You should go back in," he says as he shakes off his dick and shoves it back into his jeans.

No names. No numbers. No false pretense that we're going to try to see one another again. I wouldn't be surprised if I wasn't the only woman he fucked tonight. "Thanks for the cigarette." I almost forget that the front of my dress was covered in whiskey coke a few minutes ago. But as I adjust everything, I feel the sticky soda syrup and I'm reminded that I smell like a bar floor.

Maybe I should go home after all, or back to my hotel room to crash for the night. I've gotten what I came here for. My body feels weak from pleasure and at any moment, I'm going to leave a trail of the stranger's jizz on the floor as it drips out of me.

But when I enter Mahogany, I make eye contact with someone new. His gaze is as bright as a forest in springtime. He's not quite as tall as the man I just fucked in the alley, but he draws me to him with a crook of his finger.

I'm not the type of girl to hook up with more than

one man in a night, but something about this blonde has me oozing with lust and pheromones. Fuck convention, I guess. How do I get this man inside of me without telling him that I'm already full of another man's spunk?

VALE

PRESENT DAY

Our one night with Marilyn was perfect, or so I thought. The five of us got off and then we left. Nicodemus considered using his magic to bring us another tasty treat, but most of us were too tired. We ended up going home with our cocks tucked into our pants and another story to tell about a sexy little human that wound up with a snatch full of our juices.

Essentially, the story was over. The end had been written. Some would even say it was a happily ever after. Until the four of us looked across the courtyard and saw the silver-haired girl standing in the middle of the lawn.

I'll be the first to admit that I have an anger problem. When I get mad, I let the demon inside of me come out to play. And realizing that the four of us and Zephyrus fucked a girl at Blackwood is precisely the kind of event that brings the demon out of me.

I storm across the courtyard toward Marilyn with the other three men in hot pursuit. "Vale," Nicodemus warns, "be nice."

But all I see is red. We crossed the portal to Earth so that we could get away from everything. Our responsibilities, our connections, our abilities, our problems. We left all that in Meira'mor for one night out on the town. And now we have to face the consequences of those actions before as it turns out, we didn't leave enough behind.

"You want to tell me something, *Marilyn?*" Fire comes out of my fingertips as I approach her. With little more than five feet between us, the only thing holding me back from roasting her alive is Ares and Slade.

She laughs in my face. Then, realizing what she's done, she brings her hand up to her mouth to cover the smile. "Sorry. That was rude." Marilyn clears her throat, "You know, I thought you seemed like an asshole the other night, but now it all makes sense. You're the Devil. Of *course*, you're an asshole."

Marilyn has some big balls, I'll give her that. I've seen stronger men cower before me when faced with my wrath. "You didn't think to tell us that you were a-a-a," I fumble with trying to figure out what she is.

Her friend helps me out. "A witch," she offers with a smile.

"Jesus Christ," I close my eyes and shake my head. Of all the people from Meira'mor to fuck, I degraded myself by having sex with the weakest species known to our universe? "You're a witch? Are you visiting your mommy or daddy or something? Why are you at Blackwood?"

Ares clears his throat and gains the attention of my captive audience. "Witches are allowed at Blackwood, Vale. They're uh, they're just kind of not *good enough* to be here." He holds his hands up in Marilyn's direction. "No offense, of course. I'm sure you're powerful or whatever. Also, the other night was top-tier. Would fuck again."

I love my guys. It isn't a manly thing to say, but the five of us have been together for years. We attended school together growing up and our families were close friends. You can't spend all that time around someone and not love them. But God, what I wouldn't give to smack Ares across the face right now for bringing up what happened on Earth. "Why didn't you tell us you were a witch?" I return to the topic at hand: her betrayal.

But Marilyn doesn't see it quite like that. She lowers her hands back to her sides and sobers up. "It's not like I knew who you were. I don't just go around telling humans that I'm a witch in the event that I run into the one demon on Earth who would take me seriously." She pauses for a second before adding, "Or five demons, I guess."

Her friend shifts her weight from foot to foot, the movement seeming almost like a dance. "Wow, this is fascinating," she announces with a grin. "You guys should go on Jerry Springer or something. Do we have an equivalent of Jerry Springer? You gotta give it to the humans, that show is fucked up and fascinating. Just like this."

Nicodemus snorts behind me and when I turn to look at him, he waves me away in an apologetic fashion. I turn back to Marilyn and I can feel the anger creeping up again. Harnessing my power, I shove my hands toward her and watch as an imaginary force throws her to the ground.

"Vale!" Nicodemus hisses after a moment. "C'mon. It's the first day."

The sound of Marilyn's bones crunching as she hits the ground is satisfying. The look of pain contorting her features is almost enough to make me hard again. I have to admit that she's still beautiful, even if she is a witch and a liar.

Her eyes flash a bright shade of green, contrasting against the silver I remember from before. Marilyn is off the ground in a flash and stepping toward me as if she doesn't have a lick of fear in her system. "What's your problem?" She demands.

I don't have to tell Slade to probe the corners of her mind in search of nightmares to bring to life. I can tell from his quiet nature that he's already doing it. "You're my problem. How am I supposed to make it through the rest of the year knowing that I lowered and debased myself by having sex with a witch?"

My taunt makes her fingers flex. I watch the digits and try to figure out what her powers are. The ring on her finger makes it clear that she's a Wearer and for a second I consider trying to remove the damn thing and throwing it into the lake.

"Say that again," Marilyn glares up at me.

Why couldn't I smell the witch on her before? With her this close to my face, the scent of burning flesh fills my nostrils. She smells like her ancestors, the burned witches of days gone by. "I demeaned, cheapened, and disgraced myself by having sex with you the other night," I repeat. "For future reference, I will background check all the women I fuck from now on. You've ruined me. I hope you're happy."

"You're getting under her skin," Slade comments quietly from behind.

Marilyn looks past me and the anger in her eyes intensifies. "When The Council told me I was Blackwood Academy material, I didn't believe them. But now that I'm considering how to dismember your corpse and bury the four of you together, it makes sense." She's kind of cute when she's angry. I wonder how she'll look covered in blood.

I bring my hand up to my arm and sharply rake my nails down the skin. Nothing is left in the wake of my deep cuts, at least not on me. Marilyn jumps backward, shocked by the sudden digging of nails into her skin and the droplets of blood that appear. "I'm practically a human voodoo doll, sweetheart. Eat your fucking heart out."

Somewhere, somehow, the friend has found a lollipop. She pops it out of her mouth and interjects, waving it around like a pointer as she speaks. "This has been fun, believe me," she says with a little laugh. "But I've barely gotten to know my roomie and I'd like a little more time with her before you guys kill her and make it look like an accident. So why don't we wrap this up and come back in say, three to five business days?"

Her banter cuts the tension like a knife. She brings some much-needed levity to a situation that was fraught with unease just moments ago. I like her. If she wasn't attached to Marilyn, I might ask what she's doing later.

"I don't need to waste my time on the likes of her anyway," I decide. "It's clear that in three, maybe four months, she'll manage to stumble into killing herself without any help from me. Witches don't belong at

Blackwood. They're weak and better considered a circus sideshow. Take your little pet and go."

The tall one slips the lollipop back into her mouth and shoots me a wink. "If I had a pet demon, I'd take it outside and shoot it. At least my pet witch can do tricks. You're just a biblical creature with an anger problem." She fakes a sad face and then grabs Marilyn's hand. "Too-doo-loo, handsome."

Watching them retreat makes my blood boil. There's a witch at my academy, a witch that I fucked, no less. And her scrappy little roommate disrespected me. What the hell is happening this year?

NICODEMUS

Red dress. Big tits. Silver hair. She stands out from everyone else in the club. The second I saw her, I knew that she would be ours. "That's the human," I tell the boys, "that's the one I'll work my magic on."

In Vale's eyes, I see lust. I don't need to change his biochemistry in order for him to be attracted to her; he is already ready and raring to go.

Zephyrus has a little frown on his forehead and I can feel his worry bumping into me like a curious child. "Are you sure she's old enough?" He hesitates. "She looks-"

"-perfectly fine," Ares finishes for him with a growl and a grin. "Wanna tag team her?" He nudges his brother. "I'll even let you have the pussy. I just want to bury my dick between her tits and-"

"Don't be so crass," Zephyrus interrupts with a glare. "Maybe it's because I'm older, but she looks a little young to me." If by oldest he means twenty-seven, then yes, he is the oldest of the group. The rest of us are still attending Blackwood Academy, but he graduated two years ago. He likes to lord it over us that he's a distinguished, respectable professor teaching Dark Alchemy now, but we only razz him about it.

"She's at least eighteen," I assure the rest of them. "This district is very strict on carding." And since she doesn't have a drink in her hand, I can only assume that she's under twenty-one. The human universe and its rules about alcohol are so strange.

Vale waves his hand at me with a bored look on his face. He doesn't say anything else because he assumes that's enough. The gesture means to get on with it, do my thing, and make the human horny so we can get our rocks off.

He's never quite taken my magic seriously. As a man with dangerous, dark, demonic powers, Vale thinks that his ability to destroy and create chaos is more important than manipulating the human body. But without me, he wouldn't be watching the silver-haired girl knowing that she would fuck all of us tonight without question. He'd have to charm her, maybe even ask her his name. Vale hates getting to know humans; he should be thankful for my powers.

I tread past her carefully, skirting her line of vision.

I just need to touch her and the deed will be done. All it takes is my hand sweeping across the small of her back for me to change the chemicals in her body. A hint of estrogen to drive her wild with lust. A dash of dopamine and serotonin to increase attraction. A high dose of oxytocin to mediate her attachment to us. I dabble with a few other chemicals, but by the time my hand tears from her body milliseconds later, she is ours.

I feel her interest pique immediately. Her eyes dilate as she looks around and when someone offers to get her a drink, she accepts. He's hardly an attractive man, but the rush that she's feeling from the hormones must put that aside. She's hot and needy for a man now. We just have to step up and direct her attention to us.

Vale is first on the floor. He watches the interaction between our silver-haired, curvy queen with eyebrows knit together in consternation. When the stranger tosses his drink on her, he finds his in. "It's my turn, gentlemen." Without a look back, he takes our prize off the dance floor. The four of us watch wistfully as they disappear into the back.

"They're going outside," Ares says after a moment. "I followed them." He's a Shadow Walker. He must have slipped from shadow to darkness to see where they went. And quickly enough that Slade, Zephyrus, and I didn't notice. Or perhaps that was because our eyes were physically trained on the couple walking away, wishing that it was our turn to be with her.

Slade turns away from the direction of their exit and settles his gaze on the crowd once more. He's probably searching through their latest dreams in hopes of finding a nightmare to play on. As a Dream Bender, his greatest joy in life is living in the fantasy worlds of other people's minds. That is, perhaps, why there are always bags beneath his eyes. While the rest of us sleep, Slade dabbles in their fears.

Little chat happens in Vale's absence. The rest of us are keyed up as we wait for our chance with the human. We came to Mahogany tonight with the sole intention of giving one woman the experience of a lifetime. But it's different when we all take a turn versus ganging up on her in the bedroom.

When she walks through the door and reenters the club, I feel her presence like a draft of wind; it chills me to the bone. I catch her eye and watch as she licks her bottom lip, heart pounding in her chest when she takes me in from head to toe.

"My turn," I say loudly enough for the others to hear. I step toward her and feel tingling in my fingertips. "Nico," I greet when I approach.

She tilts her head to look up at me and a smile plays on her lips. "Marilyn."

The race is on. I won't get to her as quickly as Vale

did, but I'll give her something she won't forget. "Dance?" I ask.

"Yes," she responds. Our four-word love story; I'll remember it forever.

I grab Marilyn by the hand and pull her into me, relishing the way her body feels against mine. I can smell Vale on her, but it doesn't bother me. We've shared before. We'll share again. I think every time the five of us come to Earth and seduce a human, it brings us closer together. It's a bonding experience. Five demons, one woman, the perfect combination.

I dance with Marilyn across the floor, injecting small amounts of pheromones into her with each step that we take. Her eyes, a bright silver in the dimly lit dance club, are fully dilated. She presses her chest against me and even moans when I grab her ass. She is overwhelmed by the chemicals coursing through her veins. Every touch sets her on fire.

"Have you ever fucked on a dance floor before?" I whisper in her ear. Her shock pushes back against me, rippling through her body like a tidal wave.

Marilyn's lips part and then snap closed almost as quickly, but one more spin across the floor makes her brave. "There's a lot of people around," she observes with a raised eyebrow. "A lot of people who might see us."

I stop in place, holding onto her hips. "Isn't that part of the fun? The thought that at any second someone beside us might pay closer attention and notice that we're being more intimate way than they'd ever imagined?"

Fear slides down her throat as she swallows. I can smell it. "I'm not usually this kind of girl," she says with hesitation in her tone.

None of them are. We've never chosen a human that would ordinarily fuck five men back-to-back; women like that are hard to find. That's why we pick our targets carefully. When Marilyn wakes up tomorrow, she won't know what came over her.

"Be this kind of girl for me, Marilyn." I slip my hands down to cup her ass. "Let me be the guy who gives you an experience you won't forget." One last infusion of estrogen and dopamine push her over the edge.

She stands on her toes and presses her lips to my collarbone, leaving a red imprint in her wake. "What if we get caught?" Marilyn asks breathlessly.

I hoist her up and wrap her legs around my waist. She feels as light as a feather. I could hold her all night and never get tired. "Then we get caught, someone will probably call the cops. Dangerous, isn't it?"

Marilyn reaches between us to start unbuttoning my jeans. She knows exactly what to do. "I've never done it so publicly before," she admits with a smile. "But who's looking anyway?"

She's right. The men are too busy focusing on

women, trying to figure out which one is the most vulnerable so they can con her into bed tonight. The women are too busy sorting through the men, trying to determine if they'll have to lower their standards if they want to wind up with someone when the bar closes. Nobody looks at us, nobody except the four demons standing on the sidelines.

I make eye contact with Zephyrus and toss him a wink. His cheeks pinken with embarrassment at being caught. Slade is the opposite. He watches brazenly, his hand on the front of his jeans rubbing his cock. Vale only smirks.

"Fill me up, Nico," Marilyn whispers into my ear. She pulls aside her panties and directs my cock to her entrance.

When I slip inside her slick center, my grip on her tightens subconsciously. Despite just having thick dick Vale inside of her, she's as tight as a drum. "Damn, baby," I growl in her ear, "you're going to make me cum before I even have a chance to fuck you."

A giggle escapes her lips and she's about to say more until I start moving inside of her. Back and forth, seesawing my member through her already soaked center. Marilyn presses her forehead against me and tries to move her body in time with mine. I feel the press of her heels against my back as she rides me.

We hide our moans in the crescendo of the music. I can feel it when she orgasms, her body is flooded with natural oxytocin and prolactin. Not to mention the walls of her pussy clench and unclench as she tosses her head back and screams my name. If we weren't engulfed by a crowd, if the music wasn't blaring, everyone would know that I'd just satisfied her. Instead, it's just between the two of us. And four demons standing off to the side watching with jealousy.

It takes me another moment before I fill her. I take the crest of my pleasure from the emotions that she's feeling. I hold her in place as I shoot my load inside of her, washing away Vale's juices with my own. Anyone else would be disgusted, but the two of us have shared more than a woman before. In our formative years, we shared touches that we never speak of. We found ourselves on dark nights, veiled behind closed doors as we searched for passion and pleasure.

"No one noticed," Marilyn says after a moment.

It's difficult to pull myself out of her in this position. My prick is sensitive and a few droplets of my cum land on the floor. "Someone noticed," I whisper, low enough that she doesn't hear it. "You're quite a woman, Marilyn." This I say loudly enough for her.

She grins up at me and then brings her hand to my cheek. "You're a strange man, Nico." She doesn't even know the half of it.

"Go clean yourself up," I order. Marilyn follows the

instruction, turning her back on me and heading for the bathroom.

I walk over to Vale, shaking my head. "You could have warned me that you didn't use protection," I tell him with a roll of my eyes.

Ares' eyebrow raises. "Did *you* use protection?"

I forgot about the Bloodstone brothers and their penchant for licking a woman clean after the deed is done. "No," I admit, "but technically, we don't need to." I can no longer chastise Vale for coming inside of her when I did precisely the same thing. But the truth is that we don't have to worry about impregnating a human woman. They don't have a womb that can viably sustain a demon's baby. Even if some of our sperm attached themselves to her eggs, nothing would form.

"We gotta go," Slade says hurriedly.

Before I even have a chance to look back, the Bloodstone twins are gone. They beeline across the dance floor straight for the restrooms. "Do you think it's weird that the two of us just came in that woman and now the two of them are going to lick it up?"

Vale shrugs his shoulders. "They like what they like, I can't blame them for that. Besides, they'll get off, too."

I'm not worried about that. Of course, they'll get off. On a night like tonight, where we've chemically overloaded a human for our own pleasure, the only thing I'm worried about is breaking her. There's always a chance when you manipulate someone's biochemicals that you will fuck them up forever. Here's hoping Marilyn's perfectly fine after we're done with her.

MARILYN

PRESENT DAY

My nerves are shot through, twisted, and burned at the ends. Lilith's hand holding mine is the only thing that seems to steady me as we make our way across the lawn. "Just keep walking," she says with a smile pinned tightly to her face.

I put one foot in front of the other and force myself to keep going. The droplets of blood on my arm from Vale's attack are sliding down my skin like rain. "I need to bandage this up," I mumble more to myself than to Lilith.

She pokes her head forward to take a look before shrugging. "It isn't that bad. The dripping blood could give you a dangerous vibe in the dining hall. Like, don't fuck with me just because I'm a witch. Ya know?"

My eyes feel like they're bulging out of my head when I look at her. Lilith feels like a cool girl, the kind that everyone would want to be friends with. She's easygoing and laidback and even the demon horde seemed like they weren't willing to mess with her. "All the same," I shake my head, "I'd like to at least cleanup."

Lilith gives me a frustrated sigh as she leads me through the front door of Forge Hall. "Are you going to be like this in the Warrior Center? Because I've been known to get a little out of control when shifted. If you get burned, are you going to need immediate medical attention or can you at least finish the drill?" The bitch from our bedroom has returned.

"I would never do that to you," I respond, tone dripping with sarcasm. "Where is this Warrior Center you speak of, anyway? I didn't see it on my walk to the village." But to be fair, there were a few buildings I missed. It isn't like I gave myself a tour.

She directs me to the nearest bathroom and releases my hand. While I start grabbing paper towels and getting them wet, she hops up on the counter and kicks her legs back and forth. "So, it's not actually a building or anything. It's this clearing of land in the forest. Some of the nearby trees provide a little shelter from the elements, but I think having to battle in the heat, rain, and sometimes snow is part of the fun for the Headmaster."

Applying the wet paper towels to my cuts makes my skin burn. I grit my teeth to keep the pain from hissing out. "We have to fight in the rain?"

Lilith watches as little blood droplets appear on the skin that I just cleaned. Her nostrils flare as she breathes in deeply, taking in the scent of iron. "Yeah. Rain can be counterproductive for some races. Specifically, me. My vision isn't that great under normal circumstances, but I'm pretty much flying blind during bad weather."

We all have our weaknesses, it would seem. I chuck a wad of bloody paper towels into the trash can and grab some dry ones to start the process all over again.

"So, how about the Blackwood Five, huh?" Lilith tentatively brings up the reason we're in this bathroom. "You sure know how to kick off a new year with a bang."

I shoot a glare in her direction, none too pleased with her double entendre. "I'm never going to Earth again, I can tell you that," I mumble.

"Did you really sleep with all of them?" For a second, I have to meet her eyes to check and see if she's judging me. The hesitation in her question makes me think that she doesn't think too highly of what I've done. But all I'm met with is genuine curiosity.

I give her a little sigh as I continue cleaning up my

wounds. The blood slows with every application of the wet towels. "Sleep is an operative word. I had sex with them. All of them." I'm looking at the ground when I roll my eyes. It sounds bad when I say it out loud.

The morning after it happened, I woke up in a hotel room alone. I felt strangely satisfied, despite the fact that I'd just added five men to my body count. It was the kind of story Cassandra would have been interested in hearing. She'd pop a bag of popcorn and get herself a mug of tea while I spilled my tea. But I didn't tell her what happened. In fact, I didn't tell anyone what happened. It was a secret that I kept to myself. A filthy, delicious little secret that I swore I would take to the grave.

"I'd be careful if I were you," Lilith says after a few moments. "Not just because the five of them are crazy, either. And believe me, that little taste you got from Vale will seem like kisses compared to what he's capable of."

There isn't a first aid kit lying around. There are no bandages for me to dress my wound with. So I grab another handful of paper towels and dab at the scratches one last time. "Had I known what they were," I frown for a second before changing my tone, "had I known *who* they were, I wouldn't have done it. That's not something I normally would have done anyway, but I felt weird that night."

Lilith's eyes grow two sizes as she straightens her

back and snaps her fingers together. "I bet Nicodemus did his thing," she announces proudly like a detective that's solved the case.

I try to remember what she told me about Nicodemus. The pretty boy. Something about genetics? "What is *his thing* exactly? Remind me."

"Biochemical manipulation."

What big words she uses. All the better to ruin a life with. "I guess that would make sense. I wouldn't ordinarily let a pair of twins fuck me in a dirty club bathroom unless someone was performing some kind of magic on me." That's kind of the truth. I've had sex in a bathroom before, but it was with one guy and the bathroom in question was noticeably cleaner.

Lilith sticks her tongue between her teeth with a big smile on her face. "Wow, get it, girl. How were Ares and Slade? Specifically, Slade. That man gives me the creeps."

If I would have known at the time that he had a penchant for using a person's nightmares to mess with them, he might have given me the creeps as well. "He was fine. They were all fine. Well," I pause to dig for a better word, "it was some of the best sex I've ever had. I didn't talk to them much, hence why none of us shared the convenient little fact that we are all from Meira'mor."

She shrugs her shoulders. "You win some, you lose some."

"You're telling me," I reply with a snort. "It was good though. All of them are very different. Even Ares and Slade." I test their names on my tongue and they feel heavy and foreign. Before today, I was happy to remember them as good-looking strangers who'd done dirty, dirty things to me. Now they have names and histories and I can't really get behind that. "I'd like to forget it though. I don't want any trouble." If the rest of them are anything like Vale, trouble is all I'm going to be faced with.

But Lilith has another take on it. She nods her head wisely in agreement with me before hopping off the counter and searching for something to do. "It's against the school rules anyway," she offers with a pliant smile. "The more distance you put between yourselves, the better."

School rules? We're all adults. "What rules?" I ask with a frown. "We can't date? What else can't we do? Have sex? We're in our twenties. I didn't sign up to be celibate."

Lilith walks to each of the three stalls in the bathroom, pushing the doors open to reveal that no one is inside. While she moves from door to door, entertaining herself, she talks. "No, don't be absurd. You can date whoever you'd like." Lilith pauses to purse her lips before adding, "Well, *you* can't. There are no other witches or wizards here."

It takes a second for the information to dawn on

me. When it does, I chuck the rest of the paper towels in the garbage and straighten up. "You mean we can't date outside our race? That's a little, well, for lack of better words, racist."

She flashes me an apprehensive look before leaning up against a wall. "Blackwood probably doesn't have a problem with someone like me dating someone like Vale. They probably wouldn't care if I switched teams and dated a succubus, either. But, well," Lilith shrugs, "you're a witch. When it comes to relationships and reproduction among your race, the rules are different. You guys aren't allowed to cross-breed. You know that, right?"

I've heard the rules plainly stated all my life. All marriages between witches and other races are done with supervision from a special team of Meira'mor's doctors. Because of our biological makeup, some witches have the power to absorb magic from their partners. When they're other witches and wizards, it doesn't quite matter. But when they're with a shifter or an elemental, things can get a little hairy. "Have no fear. I have no interest in breeding." At least not anytime soon. I need to figure out if being a mom is in the cards for me. After my *exemplary* show of parenting while growing up, there is a chance that I might not be a suitable maternal figure.

"Good," Lilith breathes a sigh of relief. "Because the Headmaster wouldn't hesitate to expel you if he knew about what happened between you and the Blackwood Five. The whole sex thing," she adds, "not the fight in the yard. He wouldn't care about that. But he might even go as far as to talk to The Council about having your magic stripped if he knew you had sex with them."

I shudder just thinking about it. Having ones magic stripped is a dangerous process. Every few years we hear a story on the news about someone dying from the procedure. It's a rare occurrence, but it's possible. "I guess we witches really are hated around here." I joke to mask my fear. Could a dalliance across the portal really lead to my death?

MARILYN

3 WEEKS BEFORE

There's nothing wrong with hooking up with two men in the same evening. That's what I tell my reflection but she doesn't seem too convinced. Her eyes look a little skeptical and her hair is a bit askew. The glow on her face tells me that she's been thoroughly fucked and she's exhausted. I think it's time to call it a night.

I finger-comb my hair to make it a little more presentable and start making a to-do list. Clean myself up. Get an Uber. Go back to the hotel. Sleep until it's noon. Head back—

My list is interrupted by a knock on the door. Someone twists the handle, but thankfully, I had the foresight to lock the door behind me. "Occupied!" I yell at the potential intruder. "It'll be a minute." But the knocking only grows louder. It sounds like multiple hands are on the door, all of them banging on the wood as if they're going to tear the door off its hinges.

"Jesus," I swear under my breath, "can't even wait a God damn minute for a girl to pee." I didn't even get a chance to grab a tissue and wipe the come dripping down my thighs, either. "Didn't you hear me?" I ask with an attitude as I pop open the door. "It's occupied." The tail end of my sentence drops off as I see two identical-looking men standing before me. "Um, this is the ladies' room?"

God, I'm a sick and perverted person. Because looking at these two handsome men, I feel a flutter in my stomach. Or is the flutter down lower? *It wasn't enough to fuck two strangers in the last hour, you want to double the number?* The little voice in my head asks like the bitch she is. She reminds me of my mother, which is probably why I ignore her.

The shorter of the two, with black hair cut short and styled with gel, leans against the door frame with a smirk on his face. "I don't think you're a lady."

My eyebrows raise in shocked response. "Excuse me?" The audacity of these two.

The other twin wears his hair long. He reaches forward to drag his fingers down my cheek and I feel my heart race at the touch. "We saw you on the dance floor with the blonde," he says with a knowing smirk.

A lump rises in my throat. I didn't see either of

these two men around us when Nico and I were bumping and grinding a little too closely. I hold my head high and cross my arms over my chest. "Yeah, I was dancing. What of it?"

The brothers exchange a glance. "Is that what they're calling it these days? I've heard of dancing between the sheets, but the two of you were getting mighty comfortable in front of the whole club."

So they did see. I wonder where they watched from. "Listen, I'm not usually the kind of girl that—"

The taller of the two places his hand on the half-opened door and shoves it open. The strength of his push causes it to crack as it slams into the wall. "We want a turn, beautiful. Ares over here wants to lick that pussy of yours clean. It's kind of his thing," he says with a bemused shrug.

My jaw drops open at the request. I should be in shock, but instead, I'm aroused. My body is doing things today that I never thought it was capable of. "I-I don't know," I can feel my heart start to pound in my chest as the excitement builds up. I know what the lady inside of me should do. She should tell these men to take a hike. But tonight, the lady inside of me has been dormant.

Ares takes a step in my direction, driving me further into the bathroom. "It'll feel good, baby, trust me." His brother follows, shutting the door behind them. I hear the lock click and the heat in the bathroom increases by ten degrees.

This isn't normal. I know that humans find me more attractive than their interspecies counterparts, but this isn't the usual response I get when I come to Earth.

I keep walking backward until I hit the sink. The feeling of the cold, wet porcelain seeps into my dress. "Oh," I jump, startled by the sudden distraction.

Ares falls to his feet. "Come on, honey. Let me pull those panties down and clean you up for my brother."

My skin is on fire. I want to tell them no, but I can't. And I know that deep down, it's because I don't want to. These black-haired, hazel-eyed twins are offering me the opportunity of a lifetime. And I'll be damned if being a good girl is what stops me from taking advantage of the experience.

His eyes meet mine from the ground. Slowly, he reaches up, hands disappearing beneath my dress until they reach the waistband of my panties. Honestly, they weren't much use tonight anyway. I've just been pushing them aside and having them pulled down. What was the point of wearing them?

Ares slides the fabric down my thighs slowly as if waiting for me to tell him to stop. But when I don't and he reaches my knees, he snatches them off faster. "God," he swears as he spreads my legs and takes a deep whiff of my center, "you smell like walking sex."

Do I tell him that that isn't just one man's cum? That just before I fucked Nico on the dance floor, I had a quick little thing with some guy in an alley? Does that matter to a man like him?

The answer to that question never surfaces. Ares buries his tongue inside of me and I have to grab onto the sink to keep from falling. My thighs quiver as the handsome man before me cleans away the evidence of my behavior this evening.

"Look at me," the other twin says. He runs a hand through his hair, pulling the dark locks away from his eyes. I'm met with a muddled green and brown, the pattern of which I'll never forget. "Watch me, gorgeous."

My eyes slip to his waist when I see him messing with his belt. My body feels like it's a thousand degrees as Ares swirls his tongue inside of me, but his brother is tantalizing my other senses.

He pulls his cock out of his pants and starts handling himself. "Do you see what you do to me?" He asks as he starts tugging on his member. "Do you see how hard you make me?" He grits his teeth. "Do you see what watching my brother clean you up *does* to me?"

I don't know what's hotter at this point: knowing that the taller one is turned on by watching us or the way Ares brings his hand up to my clit to massage it with his thumb. I'm holding onto the sink for dear life, afraid that if I let go, I'll crash to the ground.

"I need inside her, Ares," the twin says after a few more moments. "I need to feel her tight little walls wrap around me as I pump her full of my cum."

Ares disentangles himself from me, but I see a look of frustration on his face as he pulls away. "I didn't even get her off yet," he says with a glare.

The brother steps forward, hand still massaging himself as he lines up to sink inside of me. "Give me two fucking minutes and you can get her off as much as you like," he growls.

As soon as I start to think that the other twin is just here to get his rocks off, he starts jackhammering his cock inside of me. The tip of his head slams against my cervix, but he's not the first one tonight. He grabs onto my hips to hold me into place as he pounds away. Despite myself, I can feel an orgasm building. My heart throbs in my chest and I wrap myself around him to take his cock deeper.

"That's right," he whispers in my ear, "you like that, don't you, you filthy slut."

The words call to something deep and primal inside of me. I've fantasized about being with a man who knew when to call me his angel and when to tell me I'm his dirty little whore. I've never picked the right man, at least not until today.

"You're gonna take my cock," each word is separated with a thrust, "then you're gonna take my brother's. We're twins, baby. We. Share. Everything." Then he orgasms with a roar, his juices coating my insides like the other two men before him. The feeling of his cock pumping into me sends me over the edge. "Yeah, that's right. You love it when men pound you. You're a real slut for some good dick, aren't you."

It's like he's speaking my dreams into life. I throw my head back and bite my lip to keep from crying out. My thighs are twitching from the workout I'm getting in tonight.

I don't even have time to recover before Ares is pushing his way into the scene. "Fuck you," he says to his brother, "I could have gotten her off with my tongue."

At this point, I'm so blissed out from the three orgasms I've already had tonight that I don't even care that I didn't get tongue fucked. Ares has himself pulled out and he enters me with a groan. "So wet and warm," he presses his forehead against mine, "and still so tight."

I don't have it in me to orgasm again, or at least I don't think I do until Ares starts rocking back and forth gently. His movements stir the beast inside of me. After tonight, I swear she'll be dormant for years as I try to get her used to having just one man at a time from now on.

"You're taking your sweet ass time," the other brother says with a sigh.

"Shut the fuck up, Slade." Ares is bringing me back to life. Every stroke makes me moan a little louder. The other guys tonight have all fucked me hard and quick until both of us were coming. Ares is slow and methodical, bringing me to the height of my pleasure at a leisurely pace.

I wish I felt some kind of shame for what I've done. I wish that staring past Ares at his brother and making eye contact with him as I come made me feel embarrassed. But the long-haired man only winks at me and the contractions of my orgasm grow stronger. Ares bites my shoulder as he pours into my pussy, causing me to redirect my attention to him.

The creaking of the sink is what tears the three of us away from this situation. It's spent the last few minutes holding me up against the constant onslaught of being fucked. "Shit," I swear as I scramble to climb off the edge.

The bathroom isn't big enough for the three of us to be moving around so erratically. Suddenly, the space feels cramped.

"I'll leave," Slade offers.

Ares follows suit. "So will I."

Just as quickly as they came, they're gone. I'm left in the bathroom with my panties ditched on the ground, a slow leak escaping from the back of the sink, and my dignity nowhere to be found.

What happened tonight? I still can't piece it together. I came with the intention of finding a man to take back to a hotel to fuck. But somehow, it's nearly time to go home, and I'm not taking anyone with me. I've still managed to have sex, four times, in fact, so maybe I don't need to take anyone home.

I do my best to clean up. My insides feel like jello. I swear that anyone who comes within a ten-foot radius of me will know what I've been doing. I reek of sex and cum and sweat and cologne. God, I'm exactly what Slade said I was. I'm a filthy slut.

I own it though. I toss my panties into the garbage and make my way back into the club. The music seems a little louder than before. The flashing lights are now hurting my eyes. The bodies pressing against mine as I try to make my way through the crowd start to make me feel like I'm suffocating. Hot, sticky, unable to breathe. These are the fragmented thoughts that I have before it all swirls down the drain. I don't think I make it to the door before I black out. But somehow, when I come to, I'm outside.

"Are you okay?" I'm met with eyes that remind me of honey in the jar. A soft, sweet brown that makes me feel safe. "You took quite a spill back there," he says with a gentle smile.

If this is karma for fucking four dudes tonight,

then God must favor me. Because there's no way that he's giving me this beautiful man for being holy. After what I just did in Mahogany, either God's proud of me or there really is a devil looking out for selfish, sinful souls like me.

Vale shoots me a dozen looks throughout the dining ceremony. Nicodemus tries to usher me over as people pour out of Forge Hall. But Headmaster Merryweather calls me over at the last minute and I don't get a chance to see what the guys want.

"A couple of things, Zephyrus." Merryweather's eyes follow the demons out of the room. He has a jovial smile on his face as he pats students on the back absentmindedly as they leave.

I nod my head to do something, feeling a little out of place speaking face-to-face with the Headmaster when I'm not in any trouble. "Sure. What can I help you with?"

Merryweather waits for a majority of the students to exit the dining hall before he turns his full attention to me. He reaches up to fiddle with the collar of my shirt before dusting his hands down the front of my chest. He smoothes out the fabric, a strange habit for someone like him.

Everybody knows that the Headmaster is a werewolf. All you have to do is look at his hulking stature to know that he is inhumanely strong. "About your little friends," the smile on his face tightens into a pained look, "I'm going to need you to put some distance between yourselves this year. Now that you're a professor, you need to act accordingly."

There were times when the five of us were walking through the halls of the Blackwood Academy headed straight for his office. Vale had maimed someone or Slade had driven them crazy. I was once responsible for burning down half the forest. Merryweather had to ask the Silverleaf Academy to send over a few witches with ties to flora magic to regrow what I'd turned to ashes. Never were a group of five as closely bonded as Vale, Nicodemus, Ares, Slade, and I.

"When I gave you this position, it was because your alchemist abilities were far beyond that of our former professor. You seemed to understand the principles of matter better than anyone I've ever met. But perhaps," he pauses, "perhaps I should have waited a few years. Granted, our current students wouldn't be benefitting from your wisdom, but at least if I'd have waited until the Bloodstone twins were gone, you wouldn't hold any ties to the remaining students," he trails off. Merryweather picks imaginary lint off of my shirt, flicking it away with a sour look. He towers above me by nearly a foot and when he looks down on me, it makes me feel small even at 6'4".

I clear my throat and pull my shoulders back, trying to strike a confident pose. "I think that I can separate myself from my friends, Headmaster. I understand that there is a power dynamic in place now and I'll make sure that they, and myself, respect that."

A charming little smile replaces the tight one on Merryweather's face. He makes eye contact as he nods in agreement with what I just said. "Also, we have a witch at the academy this year. I don't think she'll be very difficult to deal with, but make sure to push her. I don't want her to think that just because her magic isn't as refined or as strong as other students that she can slack off."

I read between the lines: Merryweather wants me to make her time here difficult enough that she quits. Fair enough. Witches don't belong in the halls of Blackwood. I don't think that's because they're weak or ill-suited for the type of magic taught in our halls, I think it's because their souls are too pure. They are a kind-hearted race and they belong at any of the other academies. "I understand, sir," I tell him with a solemn nod.

"Good. And please, report back to me if she is a

problem or can't seem to do the work. We'd just like to keep a closer eye on her." Merryweather's tone is menacing. If I were the witch, I'd leave the academy. You couldn't pay me to subject myself to the humiliation that she will no doubt endure at Blackwood.

I never manage to connect with Vale or Nicodemus. When I exit the dining hall, I don't see them lingering in the entryway. Nor are they patiently waiting for me outside of Forge. I figure that whatever they have to say can wait until I see them in class next.

I go back to my room in the staff village and start working on how to tell the guys that I can't be too friendly with them anymore, at least not on the school grounds. On the weekends when we're off campus, we can be thick as thieves if we want.

I know that Ares will take this the hardest. Though he has his twin to confide in, sometimes when things between him and Slade get a little tense, he comes to me for advice. He calls me the older brother he never had.

The night passes into morning and by the time I wake up, I'm no closer to figuring out how to tell any of them that we need to put a little division in our friendship. But I figure that if I start to pull away a little bit, they might begin to understand. After all, none of them are stupid. They'll have to know that the friendship we had before I was a professor couldn't be the same now that I hold a position of power.

My classroom in Latham Hall is on the third floor. Students with the power of translocation and teleportation skip the stairs and appear in the classroom they're supposed to be in while I fight the students jamming up the stairwell chatting about their summer break. They all look at me funny as if I'm bothering them. I know now why alumni professors take a special staircase in the back of Latham. Regardless of how close I am in age to these kids, they don't see me as the lovable demon who once walked the halls with them.

When I finally make it to my classroom, everything is as I left it a few days before. I manually light the candles on every desk and wait for my first class to arrive. Students slowly trickle into the room in small groups of two or three. They shoot a look at me and then giggle behind their hands. They have the youngest professor in the building, how scandalous.

I make my way back to my desk to get my papers ready when I catch a glimpse of silver hair out of the corner of my eye. I'm sure it's no one that I know, so I toss a careless glance in that direction. When I see Marilyn's face—the sharpness of her cheekbones, the curve of her lips, the swell of her breasts beneath her white shirt—I choke on my spit. Not to mention I swing my hands across the desk to turn toward her and knock off a handful of items. They scatter to the ground, clattering on the marble floors. A mug breaks and sends ceramic pieces flying in every direction.

Nobody gets up to help me. The students, in fact, laugh behind their covered hands. The look on Marilyn's face is a little fearful and a little confused, but she makes her way to the back of the class without stopping to say anything to me.

That's when I hear it. Under the chuckles and conversation about who went where for the summer, I hear whispers.

"That's her," someone says, "that's the witch."

Someone else makes a retching sound. "God, she even looks like one. That hair? Please."

"She doesn't belong."

"She can't compete with us."

"She's no good."

To Marilyn's credit, she doesn't rise from her chair and tell them that she can hear them. She looks ahead, at me. We lock eyes and I'm inundated with memories of the last time I saw her.

Deep breath, Zeph, I tell myself. This doesn't have to go any farther. I can just pretend that what happened between us never happened.

It occurs to me that this might have been the reason Vale was so desperate to talk to me last night. Dread fills my stomach as I realize that if he knows she's here, she's a dead woman. He'll never forgive himself for having sex with her. He'll never forgive her for not telling him what she is.

In my revelations, I stop in place and start thinking about what this all means. Marilyn seems to think this pause means that I need help. I see her hand raise and the smattering of broken ceramic pieces lift with it. She directs them to the desk and they land with a satisfying crash. There is a wan smile on her lips, almost apologetic.

"Pfft. I could move shit with my mind when I was five," another student calls out. "That power is pathetic."

I'm about to call the class to order when the fervor grows louder.

"You don't belong here!" Another woman moans. "Go home already, witch."

"This is a *real* academy, *bitch*. Oops," he chuckles, "I meant witch."

The berating begins as if we are back in high school. The students start to gang up on her, making hateful comments about her race and her placement at Blackwood. If I'm being honest with myself, two years ago, I would have joined them. I'd have one of the guys by my side as we tore down the witch's confidence for daring to step on our campus.

But today, I just feel like an outsider looking in. I know that I should say something, but my mouth refuses to work. It's as if the hinge of my jaw needs oiling.

While I'm busy contemplating what to do and if I should step in, Marilyn is growing angrier and angrier. Her cheeks are an apple red and her eyebrow is knit so tightly in frustration that she's going to give herself wrinkles. I look at her hands and notice that they're balled up into little fists. Her grip is so tight that her knuckles are turning white. I open my mouth to call the class to order when a warp of magic hits us all.

I'm thrown to the ground along with everybody else. Desks are overturned. Papers go flying. The broken ceramic mug flings pieces in every direction. The only one left standing, or should I say sitting, is Marilyn.

Everybody else is trying to pick themselves up off the ground. Confusion is on everybody's faces, even her own. "I-I didn't mean to do that," she apologizes quickly. Her jaw refuses to close. She looks at the angry people helping each other up and can't seem to move a muscle.

I don't know what just happened here, but I know it wasn't intentional. I scramble to my feet and draw everyone's eyes toward me. "That's enough, everybody. It's time to start class. No more messing around. Get back to your desk and turn to page 32 of your alchemy textbooks."

It takes a few moments for everyone to follow the

order. The students are grabbing their books off the ground, mumbling about the stupid witch in the back, and trying to right their desks and themselves. But after an eventful first five minutes of the day, everybody settles in.

Except for me, who can't stop thinking about the burst of power Marilyn just displayed. Is this something Merryweather would want to know about? He'll find out, of course. Word of what happened here will spread fast. But should I abandon my second class of the day and head to his office? Or does my prior entanglement with this witch mean that I should be looking out for her despite what Merryweather requested?

My first day as a professor and I'm already embroiled in a scandal with a student.

Fucking goons. All of them. I told Nicodemus to stop pumping her full of hormones and pheromones and chemicals and shit, but he never listens.

I watch our silver-haired beauty disappear into the crowd. One minute she's walking to the exit, the next she's on the floor. Vale gives a little snort and remains leaned up against the wall with his arms crossed over his chest. Nicodemus doesn't even notice; he's too busy exchanging stories with the twins. I'm the one that curses under my breath and decides to save her.

"Zeph!" Vale calls after me lazily.

I ignore him as I push my way through the flood of people on the dance floor. I swear the same people that can't hold their liquor upright are the same ones who didn't wear deodorant tonight. This pack of bodies smells like unwashed gym socks.

The crowd has enough sense to back away from Marilyn when she falls. They leave a human-shaped hole around her collapsed body, each individual still moving in time with their preferred partner instead of trying to help her to her feet. God, she's going to be sticky when she wakes up. This floor has seen more soda than a kid's birthday party.

I lean down to grab Marilyn, scooping her into my arms and picking her up. The crowd parts a little more, angry eyes shooting in my direction as her feet smack against them. I dare any one of them to say something to me. But no one does. As I push my way through the crowd, everybody remains silent. Or as silent as a person can be in a club where the music is blaring at an ear-splitting volume.

Outside in the cool evening air, I walk with Marilyn to a bench half a block away from the club. She stirs a little, but her eyes don't open. When I set her down, I keep her head aloft so I can scoot in underneath and act as a pillow.

For midnight, the streets are pretty packed. A crowd of people stand outside of Mahogany waiting to get in. Every few moments, someone walks by on their way to the park across the street. They look over at us, but they don't say anything. They're too wrapped up in their own lives to interfere. Humans are a strange breed.

While I wait for her to wake, I take mental snapshots of her face. The way her eyelashes flutter in the breeze. The curve of her lips, weighted down in faded red lipstick. Her silver hair, shimmering under the streetlights. Her beauty is like a siren call, beckoning me closer. For a human, she is stunning. Everything about her is alluring.

I don't have a chance to take her in for long. Marilyn's eyes start to open and I'm met with a gaze that matches her hair. "Are you okay?" I ask as she blinks up at me. I flash her a soft, gentle smile. "You took quite a spill back there."

For a fraction of a second, she seems stunned into silence. Her eyes drift over me before she nods her head yes. "Where have you been all my life?" The question slips from her lips with a hint of a smile and I assume she's still feeling the side effects of Nicodemus' biochemical magic.

I reach up to swipe a few strands of hair out of her face. "Where do you live, honey? I'll get a cab to take you home." It occurs to me that I won't have sex tonight, but that's okay. I'm doing a good deed.

Lately, I've become disillusioned with this tradition of ours. I didn't mind it when I was a couple of years younger, but now it seems a little predatory. Maybe even illegal. Going through the portal to trick a woman into sleeping with the five of us doesn't have the hold over me that it did when I was in school.

Marilyn's tongue comes out to sweep across her bottom lip. As she pulls it back, she exchanges it for her bottom lip. I watch as the red lipstick turns a shade darker when she bites down. "I'm not from around here," she says after a second. "I have a hotel room just a couple of miles away though. I-I'm just visiting," she hesitates.

I wish I could rifle through her thoughts. I wish my magic was more person-focused. I'm accomplished in alchemy, I can make dark and dangerous things, but I can't tell if the woman before me is telling the truth. I only have her words to go off of. And the way she looks at me curiously, as if she's trying to figure me out.

"Let's get you a cab," I repeat. Whatever happens, I won't be responsible for leaving her here to fight off the side effects of Nico's magic. Or, God forbid, a more predatory male that might take advantage of her. Humans are a weak breed. If I leave her here, who's to say she won't go right back into Mahogany and fuck some other strangers?

Marilyn rises from my lap and I'm quick to get up, offering her a hand to help her to her feet. "What's the name of the hotel?" I ask as I lead her back toward the club. Cabs are coming and going at lightning speed, picking people up and dropping them off.

"Come with me," she says after a moment, her grip

tightening around mine. "I-I feel a little strange. It would be nice to have someone make sure that I get home safe."

I'm about to tell her no when I look at her and see a hint of vulnerability in her eyes; it makes me weak in the knees. All evening I've been eyeing this girl as a potential sexual partner. Now I can't see myself doing anything but taking care of her. Maybe getting her a glass of water before tucking her into bed. "Alright. I'll get you to the hotel, but I have somewhere to be in the morning. I can't stay long." I won't stay at all, in fact. I'll get her through the door and then leave.

A cab stops to pick us up and Marilyn rattles off the address. "Do you mind if I put my head on your shoulder?" She asks with a yawn. "I'm exhausted." But before I respond, she's already leaning against me. Her eyelids droop until they're fully closed and her breathing slows.

"Is she okay?" The driver asks, his eyes drifting from the roadway to the two of us in the backseat.

"She's fine," I tell him gruffly. I hope that's the truth. What if she's suffering from sensory overload? Or her body is rebelling against all the chemicals Nicodemus forced into her bloodstream? *Maybe she's just tired,* a little voice in my head says. But I know it's more than that.

I make a pact with myself right then and there: I will no longer participate in this human hunting game we invented. We were the Blackwood Five once, but not anymore. I'm a professor. I'm the most mature of the men. I need to start being the responsible one. We've got to leave the humans out of our sick and twisted games.

The cab driver watches us through the rearview mirror, eyeing me with suspicion as he pulls up in front of the hotel. "Did you drug her?" I see his fingers clutch around a cell phone in his lap. Does he think he's going to call the cops on me?

I gently prod Marilyn until she wakes up. "See?" I gesture toward her as she yawns and looks around. "She's fine."

As if realizing something unsavory is happening between the driver and me, Marilyn shoots the driver a smile as she pulls her wallet out of her bag. "Thank you. Sorry about that. I think I was a little drunker than I thought." A lie. I never saw her take a sip of alcohol.

The two of us disembark and the cab driver keeps sitting there. He's bent over the middle console, peering through the passenger side window to watch the two of us walk to the hotel. "He thinks I drugged you," I tell her quickly.

Marilyn shrugs her shoulders and heads for the entrance. "He can think what he wants. I don't care."

I follow her to make sure she's alright. We enter the lobby and the night clerk gives us a smile. Marilyn doesn't acknowledge him as she heads for a hallway leading away from the lobby. We transition from bright, chandelier lights to dim fluorescent bulbs. The rooms are spaced quite a far distance apart. The carpet feels thick and dirty beneath my feet. Some of the fibers don't quite move right as we walk and I find myself almost tripping over my own feet trying to keep up with Marilyn. "Are you going to be alright? Do you need me to get you anything? Food? Water? Some ice?" I ask as we pass by a machine.

At the end of the hall, she stops in front of the last door and pulls out her key card. One swipe against the magnetic strip and the door unlocks. "Come inside."

I should go. As she disappears into the room, the door slowly starts to close behind her. This is my chance to get out of this situation unscathed.

Except I foil myself by putting my foot out to catch the door before it locks me out here in the hallway alone. "Listen," I lean into the room and call for her, "I just wanted to make sure you got home safely. I've got to head out now."

She steps into the narrow hallway visible from the door. Except now her dress is gone and she stands there naked. "You mentioned. Somewhere to be in the morning," Marilyn recalls.

My jaw makes an unfortunate encounter with the ground. "You're not wearing any clothes."

Marilyn runs a hand through her hair, quickly

combing out the flyaways. "Yes, I tend to be naked before I get in the shower. It helps me clean all the nooks and crannies better than when I'm wearing a pair of pants or a bra."

The little voice in my head is screaming at me to get out of here before I get myself into trouble. If I don't bolt, I'm going to be dick-deep inside of her in 0.2 seconds. "Oh, sorry, I didn't mean to interrupt. I should go."

She takes a few steps closer. "You keep saying that, but here you are," Marilyn comments with a shrug of her shoulders. "Want to take a shower with me? I've been wearing whiskey like a cologne for hours now and it would help to have someone wash my back for me."

No. I need to go. I have to get back to Meira'mor. I have breakfast tomorrow with the Blackwood Academy Headmaster and I can't be late for that.

But I can't get my mouth to say any of those words. And I can't get my feet to back out of the room and take me anywhere but here. All I can do is stare at her perfect, curvy little body.

Marilyn reaches the bathroom door and steps inside, her hand holding onto the frame as she pauses to give me one last look. Her eyes are hidden beneath sweeping black eyelashes that she flutters at me. "You saved me tonight. Why don't you come inside and let me thank you properly?" Marilyn releases the door frame and disappears into the bathroom completely. A few seconds later, I hear the water turn on and the sound of the tub's curtain closing behind her.

At this point, there is no use listening to the little voice inside my head. It tries to tell me that she's still coming off an artificial hormone high from Nicodemus, but I don't care. I'm already walking into the room and letting the door slam shut behind me.

The tub curtain is made of the thinnest opaque material known to man. As I stand in the doorway, I can see her soaping up. She takes a cloth and runs it between her legs before bringing it up between her breasts. She is soapy and wet and my hard-on doesn't care if the other four guys fucked her first; she's clean now and she's mine.

Like a man in a trance, I move without telling my body to do it. My shirt somehow winds up on the floor on top of my shoes. I pull off my socks and then do away with my belt. My jeans are the last thing to go, but by then, I'm opening the curtain and stepping into the shower.

"I was hoping you'd come," Marilyn greets with a smile.

Beads of hot water reflect off her skin. There's a handrail on the far side of the tub and I have to grab onto it when I see her falling to her knees. "You don't have to—" My protests are cut off when she grabs my dick and brings it to her mouth. Between the water from the shower and the warmth from her mouth, by the time she takes my head all the way to the back of her throat, I'm trying to tell myself not to come.

Steam fills the air as the hot water beats down on Marilyn's back. She reaches around me to grab my ass with her hands, pulling me toward her face. She takes my cock so far down her throat that I swear she's going to choke. I hear a few gurgles and try to pull back, but she holds me in place.

I'll never talk badly about another human again. Marilyn's throat tightens around my member for a few more seconds before she pulls away. I see her silver eyes once more, flashing submission up at me as she holds my cock in her mouth. Oh, god, I think I might be in love with this woman.

Marilyn bobs back and forth, her tongue dragging across the underside of my dick as she moves. I should explode in her mouth and let her suck me dry, but there's another force at work. My lust to be inside of her is stronger than my desire to watch her guzzle down my juices. I manage to pull out of her mouth and my cock throbs in anger. "Get up," I growl, helping her to her feet.

Passion overtakes me. I have no control. I grab her slick body and push her into the corner, hiking her thigh up over my hip. She's limber, just like I like them.

I grab my cock and bring it to her entrance. The little voice reminds me that other men have been here tonight, but I drown out his cries with one of my own. As I enter her, I'm overwhelmed by sensation. I can't hold it together. I thrust inside of her like a monster unleashed, growing hotter under the shower's waterfall as I pull screams of pleasure from her lips.

This is real, I tell myself. This isn't Nicodemus' magic playing with either of us. He's somewhere back at Mahogany and I'm here in a shower with the silver-haired beauty. She rakes her nails over my back and I know that I'll have marks in the morning.

When an orgasm comes for us both, it's with a crescendo that will have her neighbors calling the front desk with a noise complaint.

I've been at Blackwood for less than twenty-four hours and I'm already doing things I've never done before.

Make a new friend? Check. Things seem to be going well with Lilith even if she keeps debating whether I'm a dud or not. Sometimes she seems convinced that I'm a powerful witch who will change the world. Other times she mourns the fact that her roommate is a witch that barely has the ability to move things with her mind.

Make a new enemy? Double check. I saw Vale across the dining hall this morning and he looked like he was going to kill me. So that is going well and will probably progress to something heinous and nasty rather quickly.

Piss off an entire classroom of people? Absolutely

check. The power needed to perform the stunt that I just did is off the charts. In fact, I've never done something like that before. It starts to make me wonder if I'm really the person that did it.

I spend the rest of class wondering where the power came from. I remember that just before people started flying and desks turned over, I was thinking about getting up and walking out of the room. Then power shot out of me and unfettered chaos reigned. I didn't move my hands or think about it; I just sat there like a bystander as everyone was flung to the floor.

I know they're all giving me side-eye. I might face forward and keep my eyes on the professor, but I see their heads surreptitiously glancing in my direction. I hear the whispers between people as they talk about me. I'm not blind to the pieces of paper that make their way from one hand to another every time Zephryus' back is turned. Before the school day is over, I bet everyone will know who I am and what I've done.

When a bell starts chiming in the distance, I allow my focus to break so I can pack up my things. I carefully avoid making eye contact with the menacing students around me and pray that nobody holds a grudge. It was an accident; I'm not even convinced that I'm the one who performed the magic. In fact, maybe someone in the class is trying to make me look bad.

"Miss Bayard," Zephyrus calls over the clamor of

students trying to leave, "if you could stay after for a moment, I'd like to speak with you." We're all in our twenties, but that doesn't stop half the class from saying, '*Oooo, she's in trouble!*'

I pack up a little slower, waiting for the final trickle of students to make their way through the door. A couple of guys hang back, trying to see if they can catch what Zephyrus is going to say to me.

"Have a good day, gentlemen," he announces loudly. Their stride picks up upon being caught by the professor.

I sling my bag over my shoulder and reluctantly make my way to the front of the classroom. The look in Zephyrus' eyes isn't quite as angry as Vale's from the day before. Perhaps he won't use this moment to kill me when there are no witnesses. "Listen, I'm sorry about what happened at the beginning of class. I didn't know—"

He holds up a hand to cut me off. "You don't need to apologize for that, at least not to me. It's tough being different from everyone else; it's even tougher when people openly mock you for it. I understand why you did what you did."

As air fills my lungs, it feels like I've been holding the same breath all class long. Fresh oxygen fills my chest and I start to feel better.

"About the other night though," he starts with an

embarrassed look on his face. His cheeks flush as he reaches up to rub the back of his neck.

"Oh, yes, that," I mumble. Here I was thinking that we were just going to skip past that. I'd pretend it didn't happen and everybody would forget about it in no time.

Zephyrus doesn't seem like that kind of guy though. He's wincing when he starts to apologize. "If we'd have known that you were from Meira'mor, we would never have done what we did. Not because you're a witch or anything," he says kindly, "but because, well, we just wouldn't have. We tend to uh, target, um," Zephyrus gives me an anxious chuckle, "this is going to sound bad, but we usually only go after humans because then we never have to see them again."

That makes sense. It's one of the reasons I've gone to the other side of the portal to get my kicks. There's something about seeing someone that you've had sex with in the daylight that makes you question every-thing you did in the shadows. "Honestly, it's no big deal. What's done is done. I'd like to forget it and I'm happy to never bring it up again." Especially if that means the Headmaster won't find out and try to turn me into The Council or something. "You just need to tell your little friend that I don't mean any harm and I'm not interested in a second quintet of fucking."

His eyebrows crease downward and Zephyrus

starts looking around the room. "What little friend?" He asks, the frown deepening as he goes through the Blackwood Five Rolodex. "Slade?" He guesses after a moment. "I know he's a little sadistic, but I don't think he's going to take what happened too seriously. He's a little strange, I'll admit, but he'll probably brood about it instead of take action."

Of the four that I saw yesterday, Slade looked the most uninterested in what was happening. "Um, no, not him. Vale, the big guy."

It takes Zephyrus all of two milliseconds to realize what I'm saying. "He found you first, didn't he." His eyes close as he shakes his head in disappointment, his fingers coming up to the bridge of his nose to stave off an impending headache. "Unfortunately, and I say this with the deepest and most sincere regret, I can't control Vale. None of us can. He's, well," Zephyrus stares at me with a gentle, sympathetic gaze, "he's a beast."

"Funny enough, I gathered that from his size." I'm willing to bet that there's no taming the beast.

Zephyrus winces as he nods in agreement. An awkward silence washes over us for a few moments, baptizing us in unfamiliarity. "I just want you to know that we're sorry, regardless of whatever Vale or any of the other guys said. I've already told them I won't be human hunting with them again. And after you passed out, I made Nico promise he wouldn't do that to humans anymore." A frown appears on his face again. "Well, I guess you weren't a human. *Aren't* a human," he corrects quickly.

He reaffirms my theory that I was under the influence when I had sex with the five of them. My interest in them might have been physical, but I know I'm not the kind of girl that would have sex with five dudes back to back. It just isn't my style. "It's fine," I offer gently, trying to lessen the blow of embarrassment that he's feeling. "If I would have gotten drunk, I'm sure I would have passed out anyway. At least I didn't have to deal with a hangover the next morning." Just a sore vagina that demanded an ice pack and some rest.

Another awkward pause occurs and I consider leaving for my next class. We have ten minutes to get from one place to the next and though I only need to go downstairs, a few moments to myself might help me brace for the next onslaught of unwanted attention.

"Quick question though." Zephyrus stops me before I go. "When you did that thing earlier, you said that you didn't mean to. I'm sure this is rude to ask, but what kind of powers do you have? If it helps," he offers politely, "my abilities are predominantly item-based. I have a knack for transforming an item's matter and creating potions, some elemental transmutation," he babbles on, "but I'm not much help in a fight. What you did earlier would be incredibly useful in hand-to-hand combat. Which, as I'm sure you know, is something that Blackwood Academy takes very seriously."

Everybody knows it happens and nobody does anything to stop it. Fascinating. "I can move and control items. My power is pretty dependent upon my ring though." I flash the silver on my left hand. "But I'm not very advanced."

Zephyrus raises an eyebrow and then starts to laugh. "That's a joke, right?" Thinking that I'm joking around seems to relax him. "What you did at the start of class was advanced for a first year. Hell, it's something that some people don't even master until their third year of academy. You didn't just move one or two items in a general direction. You upended desks, forced people to the ground, and had things driven from you like some kind of force field had been put in place."

As I hear him say it back to me, it sounds even more powerful than I originally thought. All I can do is shrug my shoulders and tell him that I've never exhibited power like that before. "Not to mention I don't know how it happened. I wasn't even thinking about it," I admit. "One minute I was considering leaving the class and the next you were all on the ground. It's like the magic exploded out of me. I had no control."

The more I talk, the deeper the frown on Zephyrus' brow seems to crease. "Interesting," he mumbles after a moment, "Just so we're clear, you've never performed any kind of magic at that level?"

My mom told me once that I developed magic in the womb. She could feel a tickle of power whenever I kicked around her belly. I never quite knew what that meant, but as the years passed, my abilities grew stronger. I could summon toys, starting with dolls and stuffed animals. As I got older, the items my magic could latch onto were larger. Once I even moved a car. Not to anywhere malicious, just across a parking lot while I was waiting for my dad.

When The Council had my ring made, I noticed a new energy when I wore it. I could grab multiple items. Like two books on a shelf or a few bags of groceries. I felt stronger as the days passed and Black-wood would help me grow that magic even more. But I'd never done anything quite as advanced as what happened before. "No," I solemnly respond, "not until today."

Zephyrus' eyes trail down to my ring. I see his head tilt to the left as he examines the silver. "Very interest-ing," he says to himself. "You can go, Miss Bayard. I'll talk to the guys about what happened across the portal. You have nothing to worry about."

But his words sound hollow. He has no control over the demons. How will he stop Vale from attacking me? How will he prevent his friends from letting loose the full extent of their magic on me?

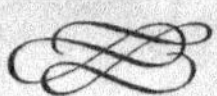

Nicodemus' room gives me anxiety.

His drapes are open rain or shine. I don't know how he sleeps in on the mornings when the sun is up by 6:00 am. Right now, moonlight shines through the window, baptizing us in silver streams. We can see the campus through the glass with nary a person walking by. Leaves flutter in the breeze, threatening to detach from the tree and take up with the lawn.

There's a fireplace in Nico's room, too. He told the rest of us that it was his reward for winning in the Warrior Center his first year at Blackwood, but I don't know anyone else who has a fireplace in their room.

His roommate is never around, not even on the nights that we stay up late drinking and discussing wild plans of world domination. It's as if Nico banished him to another realm. Earth, perhaps. Or somewhere beyond the mortal coil.

Nico's side of the room is dressed in bright shades of red and orange. He says it's because he loves fall and sunsets the best, but the pattern makes it hard to look at his side without cringing.

"Take a seat, Slade," Nico waves from the sitting area in front of the fireplace.

Ares is perched closest to the flames. For a demon, for anyone really, he is surprisingly cold at all times. Even now he's wearing a scarf wrapped tightly around his neck while he warms his hands. He says it's because living in the shadows is a cold place to be.

Vale is brooding in an oversized chair. His brows are knit together and he holds a glass full of amber liquid that he barely touches. I know what haunts his dreams. What I don't know is why it haunts his days, too.

Nicodemus has his feet kicked up on the couch, his large frame taking up the whole space. He's a little tipsy from three fingers of bourbon. He's the only one who doesn't seem phased by all this.

I approach with caution. One wrong move and Vale could snap. His energy throws me off balance and behind his dark blue eyes, I can see a storm of dreams. He likes to say that he can feel me prodding around in his head, but that must not be true. Tonight he doesn't even shoot me a cursory glare to warn me against pressing further.

"Did Zeph tell you what the meeting was about?" Ares asks.

I take a seat near the back of the pack, separating myself from them. They seem to get the point with a shake of my head and a shrug of my shoulders. "He just said that he'd be here when he can." I think we all know what he wants to talk about though. We've heard the rumors.

Vale fingers the whiskey in his hand. His grip on the rocks glass is so tight that his knuckles are turning a pale white. "How powerful is this witch, anyway?" He grumbles. It's a rhetorical question; he doesn't want any of us to answer him. The tension in the room is at an all-time high. With the exception of Nicodemus who starts to sing sailor songs from centuries past. "Do me a favor," Vale glares at his friend, "and shut the fuck up."

Nicodemus closes his eyes and lifts a middle finger. On and on he sings, not worried for a moment that his best friend might shift to demon form and challenge him to a duel.

Luckily, Zephyrus arrives before the song wears on us all. Nicodemus stops mid-verse when he hears the door opening, his words becoming less sing-songy and more excited. "Zeph," he greets with a sloppy grin, "glad you could join us."

The solemn look on Zephyrus' face says that he doesn't feel the same. I remember a time two years ago, just before he graduated, when I spent a night in his dreams. He thinks about the future a lot and he worries considerably more than the rest of us. His dreams were haunted by accolades he'd never received and hopes that he felt were out of his reach. I feel like the most introspective of the five, but I've got nothing on Zephyrus.

"Sorry I'm so late," he apologizes as he shuts the door behind him. "I had to get some paperwork completed for tomorrow's class."

Vale shoots him a glare, cutting Zephyrus' complaints off with just a look. "Get to the point. It's about *her*, isn't it?"

Zephyrus takes in the scene. He looks at the placement of the four of us, then spies the glass in Vale's hand. He is as smart as the Headmaster suggested; he knows immediately that he's walked into a danger zone. "It's about Marilyn, yes," he nods his head slowly and walks over. "What's your problem with her, anyway?"

He asks the question to which we've all been dying to know the answer. Even Nicodemus perks up, sobering long enough to find out what his friend has against the silver-haired beauty we all christened across the portal not too long ago.

I wonder if he'll say it. I've seen her dancing across his dreams for over a fortnight. Before we knew who she was, before we knew what she was, Vale dreamt about her. Summer nights where the two of them would languidly make love. Winter days where he kept her warm with the heat of his being. Dates across the portal.

But he doesn't say that. A faint red glow in his eyes suggests Zephyrus' question has awakened the demon inside of him. "She lied to us, Zeph. And she's a filthy little witch." His anger comes from a place of discomfort. One fuck with a human on Earth's side of the portal and he found himself falling for her like a damn prince from a fairytale. Love at first sight; it makes him sick. Do the other guys know that?

Zephyrus coolly mentions the obvious. "It isn't like we told her the truth either, Vale. Be realistic."

The glow in Vale's eyes grows and the hair on the back of my neck stands up. It's been a while since anyone in the Blackwood Five fought one another. We used to be hotheads when we were younger, but we've matured. At least I think we have.

"You think you're so smart because you got a big boy job," Vale spits, "but you're nothing more than a glorified science teacher."

Vale turns ugly when he's mad. While the rest of

us carefully avoid cutting one another to the bone, Vale is different. He lines up the kill shot and pulls the trigger.

We're all so used to this that Zephyrus is barely even phased. In fact, he rolls his eyes and sits on the arm of the couch above Nicodemus' feet. "That insult might be a little more hurtful if you hadn't used it before. Twice." He handles Vale's anger better than I would have. I'd have sulked in the corner and shot back when Vale was asleep. We're all different when faced with conflict and I admire Zephyrus for not bothering to back down.

Before the unspoken leader of the pack has a chance to retort, Zephyrus asks if we heard about what happened in his classroom earlier today. "I'm sure it's common knowledge by now," he says with a shrug.

By my third class of the day, I'd heard the story told half a dozen ways. Someone said Marilyn lit the classroom on fire. Someone else said she threw a desk out the window. The variations continued throughout the afternoon until the only thing I was certain of was that Marilyn had done something that pissed a lot of people off.

"Yeah, it's getting around." Ares scoots closer to the fire, bringing his hands up to taste the heat on his skin. "Did she really dangle you out of the window?"

This makes Vale snort, diverting a flash of his anger. "God, I hope so. I'd pay to see that."

Zephyrus ignores him. "No, nothing like that. She just flung everybody away from her with some kind of force field magic. Desks, papers, people," he shakes his head in confusion, "she just repelled all of it. But the kicker?" Zeph pauses and lets his eyes scan across the room. He meets everybody's gaze, looking at us all with the intent of garnering our full attention. "She's never done that before. Her magic, her powers, whatever that ring of hers can pry from the depths of her soul," he pauses, "it's never been this powerful."

That doesn't mean much to me. In fact, it sounds like a load of horseshit. She probably lied to him. There's a reason The Council saw fit to send her here. Their power is legendary, full of ancient magic that the rest of us will never develop or begin to understand. Surely one of them has foresight. Perhaps they knew all along that she'd meet us. Perhaps they know what will happen when Vale finally decides to threaten her life.

"What's that even mean?" Nico asks.

Vale understands though. He has a rare insight into magic and magical beings. "It means she's growing stronger." Is that disappointment I hear in his tone?

Zephyrus turns to look at me, asking if I've toyed around in her dreams. It's only been one night, two if you could right now. But I don't know if Marilyn is sleeping. "There's something strange about her. It's as if there are two dreams happening simultaneously. I've never seen anything like it before."

As I finish, the sound of glass shattering draws our attention. "Jesus fucking Christ," Vale swears, the whiskey that was once in his glass now strewn across the fireplace wall. "She's a witch, guys. She can attract and repel. She isn't some all-powerful being. We're giving her pesky little powers too much weight."

Nobody gets up to clean the broken glass. Vale is on his feet, pacing back and forth. I've never seen him so worked up, at least not over a woman. "Her dreams, or whatever state of mind it is that you live in," Vale glares at me, "is probably different because of her race. It can't possibly be because she's some almighty force. She. Is. A. Witch." Each word is punctuated with his anger. I can feel heat radiating off of him.

I'm not going to argue. Not because I'm afraid of Vale, but because I don't have a good argument. I don't know what Marilyn is or what she's capable of. I barely know her. She was our one-night stand that went bad. But is it strange that she's manifesting power she's never had before? Yes. And is it weird that she's having two dreams at once? Absolutely. What can I do about it though?

"Whatever she is or isn't," Zephyrus, the voice of reason, starts, "we need to keep an eye on her. The Headmaster wants her out of here."

"I want her out of here," Vale interrupts.

Zephyrus pretends as though it didn't happen. "But she was sent to Blackwood for a reason. Maybe there's more to her than a history of weak magic."

"I doubt it." Vale summons the pieces of his broken glass and chucks them into the fire. "I really fucking doubt it."

MARILYN

The Headmaster never calls me into his office. I hear rumors that I'm going to get expelled, but when nothing happens, I breathe a sigh of relief. The relief only lasts for a few hours.

People whisper behind their hands about me. I see them tighten their circles as I walk by. They giggle about the witch who almost got herself thrown out of the academy on the first day of classes, but they never talk to me. The only person who does is Lilith.

She tells me about her day. She tells me about the boys who are interested in her. She tells me the rumors she's heard about me. She has so much to say that it's practically exploding out of her by the time I get back to our room each day.

That isn't the only explosion I deal with. At night, Lilith wakes me up. She's cranky every time she shoves me around to stir me from my dreams. "If you want to control the temperature in the room, that's fine. But don't make it arctic."

With sweat clinging to my body, the chill of the air feels nice. But it isn't until I realize that none of the windows are open and I can see my breath in the air that I figure out what she's talking about. I'm the reason the room is so cold. I don't know how I'm doing it, but I'm changing the temperature. A few days later, it's like someone lit a furnace in the room. Lilith isn't happy when that happens, either.

Another night, she wakes me up by hitting me with a pillow. She opens her mouth to talk, but no words come out. It takes several frantic minutes for us to finally communicate. It turns out that I've muted her, like a channel on the television that was too loud for my tastes. All I can remember is going to sleep to the sound of her snoring. I was annoyed, but I rolled over and tried to cover my head with another pillow. As recognition dawns on me, Lilith is able to speak again. I don't know how I did it or how I undid it, but she's fine as she crawls back into bed and mumbles something about killing me if I ever do that again.

There isn't anyone I can speak to about this. My professors all look at me as if I don't belong. Even Zephyrus watches me with a keen gaze. I don't have any friends, least of all my roommate. After that acci-dental muting, she stopped speaking to me for thirty-six hours. At that point, the news that I was a leper was too exciting to keep to herself. Lilith broke her silent treatment to tell me that the rumor mill had struck again.

My days feel lonely if I'm being honest. My parents didn't tell me a lot of stories about their time at Hawthorne, but I remember their friends coming over for dinner. I listened to them share my mother's academy adventures or tell me about my father's bad behavior. I didn't think my experience would be exactly like theirs, but I thought I'd at least have one friend.

Instead, I walk from class to class in Latham Hall and wonder what it'd be like to succeed at Blackwood the way I thought I was going to succeed at Hawthorne. I spend hours daydreaming about what my life could be like, only to be slammed back into the reality that I am friendless and alone.

It's a pretty drab existence. In the week that passes, I find myself growing more and more intro-verted by the minute. My classes seem to go well, but that's because I don't have anything to do but study. Learn alchemy. Read about the history of Meira'mor and the Blackwood Academy. Strengthen my existing magic with professors also capable of attraction and repulsion. Introduce myself to a dozen new types of magic to see if I have any hidden abilities.

In my spare time or in between classes, I avoid the

Blackwood Five. Zephyrus is nice enough when I'm in his classroom, but he never misses a chance to tell me that I don't know what I'm doing. One day in front of everyone, he says that if I can't get my act together, he'll have me removed from his class. "You're not much of an alchemist anyway," he says with a shake of his head. His class is one of many that I attend for the purpose of determining what I'm capable of. It clearly isn't alchemy.

I see Vale on the fourth floor every day. We have almost back-to-back sessions with the same professor teaching us how to strengthen our core magic. Since Vale and I have a similar set of powers, it means we always wind up in the hallway together.

He never passes up a chance to lift me in the air and throw me against the farthest wall he can find. My bones crack, my back aches, and I'm certain that any day now he's not going to stop at throwing me into a wall. One of these days, a window is going to be open and he's going to chuck me right out of it.

But despite all the aches and pains that follow me throughout the day, as night fades into the morning, I feel fine again, as if my body is healing itself. Not for the first time, it makes me question what it is about this school that awakens new magic inside of me. I'd talk to Lilith about it, but she is caught up in her own little world. Not to mention she's as angry about the explosions of power that interfere with her existence.

My nights are filled with pokes and prods. I can feel Slade in my head as I sleep. The first night I didn't recognize what was happening, but when I mentioned it casually to Lilith on the way to breakfast, she warned me that he was probably the reason my nightmares were getting worse. "What nightmares?" I ask her. I've only dreamt of figures in the far-off distance. I always seem to be walking toward them, but I never reach them.

On night three, I see Slade out of the corner of my eye, but when I turn, he's nowhere to be found. He hides the shadows of my dreams, only peeking his head out long enough to see what's going on. He is harmless, but it seems creepy that he's always around.

If he's not following me while I'm asleep, his brother is following me while I'm awake. Lilith told me he was a Shadow Walker. I don't see him until the sun starts to set. His long legs follow me, stepping from shadow to shadow as I make my way across campus. Can he hear me when he's hidden in my shadows? Does he know that I see him? Does he care?

I am startled the most by Nicodemus. When I pass him in the halls, he smiles at me. He is polite, even cordial. One day he asks me how things are going and I start to think that this might be the turning point. Until I realize that he's messing with me.

His magic heightens my feelings of depression and loneliness. I only recognize it when we're far enough away that he can't reach me anymore. It's as though the tendrils of his power release me and I no longer feel like leaving this all behind. Vale might hurt me physically, but Nicodemus is the one I'm afraid of. The chemicals he floods my system with are enough to send me over the edge. I know it's only a matter of time until his magic sends me spiraling down a hole so dark that I can't pull myself out.

LILITH

Do you know what pisses me off? People who can't control themselves.

The Blackwood Five, for instance. If I hadn't spent as much time on campus as I did because of my parents' preoccupation with working 24/7, I wouldn't know them from Adam. But between semesters of learning basic math and English in a high school modeled after humans, I found myself at Blackwood. It was the home of my youth, the home of my adolescence. I had my first kiss at Blackwood with a twenty-two-year-old boy who probably shouldn't have been kissing a fifteen-year-old girl. I saw couples having sex in the woods, whispering incantations under their breath. I spent Halloween, Thanksgiving, and Christmas at the academy as my parents put on festivals and parties for their students. While I was stuck in their quarters, they were having the time of their lives.

The Blackwood Five used to be known as the Demon Pack. I grew up on the same side of Meira'mor as them and I remember when they were younger. They roamed the streets night and day looking for trouble. It wasn't until the Bloodstone twins joined the party at Blackwood that they got a reputation. And honestly, they were the picture-perfect gang.

Vale led them, despite not being the oldest. He had the strength, the power, the drive. His arrogance and inability to restrain himself are legendary. Everybody knows that when it comes to the Blackwood Five, the person you have to fear is Vale Nightshade.

Nicodemus took a comfortable second-in-command position. He privately called himself The Enforcer because all he had to do was touch someone and he'd have possession of their biochemistry for life. He made people do things just by filling them with serotonin whenever they thought about it. His charm makes me sick. I know what he's capable of; I've heard about what he's done.

Zephyrus spent his time reading. His magic felt stunted compared to the others. He might have been older and wiser, but his quiet, unassuming nature held him back. He shined in the classroom, not on the battlegrounds. My mother talked about him a lot. She told me that he had an extraordinary brain for science.

She wanted him to join her, but alas, the Headmaster got to him first.

Ares lived in the shadows. He and his brother had dark magic that went hand-in-hand, but Ares used his powers for fun. He listened to conversations between his professors and followed the drama of students he'd never met before. He was the goofball of the group who couldn't manage to keep his shadow walking to himself.

Slade went darker. When he realized that he could control nightmares and make a person's dreams their reality, he sunk into a dangerous place. It was his bread and butter to whip out someone's greatest fear in the Warrior Center. Why fight hand-to-hand when you can psychologically torture your opponent to death?

Individually, I can handle them. But when they're in a group, they're an orchestra of chaos, reaping havoc on everyone they come across. I didn't realize that my roommate would be the same way.

I don't have anything against witches. Despite common belief, I don't think they're powerless. It's because of a witch that I'm alive. When I was seven, I was still learning how to shift from dragon form into an acceptable day-to-day form. I wasn't paying attention one day and I got stuck mid-shift. It should have been fine. I should have thought about what I was doing and tried again.

But I was seven and instead of focusing, I freaked out.

Several hours later, my parents arrived home. I'd spiked a fever and my head lolled about from dehydration. They handled me with care as they took me to the nearest hospital. It was a kind witch that brought in a dozen potions she'd brewed. One to calm my heart rate. One to rid me of my fever. One to help hydrate me. And more. At seven years old, I thought she was an angel. She saved my life. I don't remember much of what happened, but I remember the cool taste of peppermint as I drank from her little vials.

Every race has a place in Meira'mor. Without one of them, we would fall apart. That isn't what everybody believes, but it's what I believe.

That isn't to say I was thrilled about being paired with Marilyn. Her scent as she walked into our room on the first day was a dead giveaway. When I heard her utter the cursed words that she was a witch, I considered marching to the Headmaster's office and demanding that he give me a new roommate. After all, my mother was a professor at Blackwood. Didn't that hold some weight?

I held my tongue though. I decided to give it some time. I'm an easygoing person. I can handle a curveball. But when the curveball started throwing out magic left and right with no explanation, I was sick and fucking tired of it.

I haven't gotten a full night's sleep since I arrived over a week ago. The first night, I listened to Marilyn's erratic breathing. It felt like I could hear her heart pounding from across the room. A cool 102 beats per minute.

The next few nights were bizarre. Either I woke up freezing cold or with sweat pouring off my body. One night I woke up with no idea what was happening. I could hear myself speak, but something felt off. It was like someone had their hands around my neck and was squeezing. Fear drove me to Marilyn's side of the room, certain that this was another one of her damn tricks. It was, but she swore to me that she didn't know what caused it.

All of her explanations were like that. She didn't have an excuse or a reason why, she would just look at me in horror and apologize while saying that she was sorry such a thing had happened. I tried to be accepting of my roommate's uncontrollable powers, but it was getting harder by the day.

When someone sprouts a new form of magic, it comes in waves of undefinable energy. Or at least that's what my mother tells me. I grew up with two abilities: one shifted me into a dragon and the other was something my mother called omnicompetence. She said she thought I was magic-less for years, but then one day, it clicked.

"You have an uncanny ability to know what, when,

and how to do things you've never done before. You can escape any situation, overcome any challenge, and you manage to always make the best decision even when presented with two decisions that shouldn't have a good outcome. Think of it like this," she said as she sat me down, "if the rest of us use 10% of our brains every day, you're using 100%. You are able to think your way out of, into, and around anything that comes your way."

That's not a magical ability. Or at least it never occurred to me to think it was magic. Knowing how to study for a class or remembering information I saw three years ago for two seconds doesn't feel magical. It just feels like when the gods were handing out powers, they said I'd be fine as a shifter who had a little more brain power than most.

But I have to say, if omnicompetence *is* a thing, it's useful.

I've spent more time in the Warnack Library than most. I know where the quiet little nooks and crannies are. I know where you can make out with someone and not get caught. I know where the secret room is for fifth years to study for their graduation boards.

I've spent hours among the dusty pages of this building. I devoured books at lightning speed between the ages of ten and fourteen. I've retained information about magic and practices that I will never use. I have scoured every inch of this place searching for answers to questions that I thought I would have one day.

Perhaps it's all my time spent at the library that leads me right to an old, tattered book. If you asked my mother, she would nod her head sagely and tell you it's magic that leads me to the right aisle. Maybe it's both.

But as I touch the spine, I feel a tingle in my chest. I pull the book from the shelf and dust off the cover. It is faded from centuries past, the words written in a language I can't understand. But something tells me that the answer to my roommate's problems is inside.

I flip from page to page, eyes drifting across worn ink. Half the words are missing or obscured. This book doesn't belong on the shelves anymore. Nothing can be gained from its pages.

But just as I'm about to snap it shut and put it back, I'm met with a surprising picture. I can't understand the text with its strange symbols, but the photo speaks to me. A woman stands before a fire with a swollen belly. In her arms is a bloody baby that bears horns and a tail. Despite the faded pages, its body is an unmistakable red. Chills race down my spine.

I flip through another few pages and watch as the creature grows through the pictures. It is a monster with scales for skin. It follows its mother closely. Untold magic lies within the sparks the artist drew as a representation of its powers. I wish I could under-stand what this all means.

I consider taking the book to the librarian and asking if she might be able to help me figure out what language it's in, but the answer hits me square in the chest. I don't need to understand the words. I don't need to know what the text says. Suddenly, it all makes sense.

The powers displayed by my roommate aren't her own. She doesn't know where they're coming from because she doesn't know what's happening to her. Somehow deep inside her womb is a baby. A small, demonic, crossbred baby.

The book crashes to the ground, shooting dust from its pages when it lands. Realization is a bitch.

Marilyn is pregnant by the Blackwood Five. She's going to have a twisted half-witch, half-demon child. God help us all.

MARILYN

When I get back from classes for the day, I find a white envelope on our dormitory door. In loopy cursive are our names: Marilyn Bayard and Lilith Valentine. My stomach flip-flops as I tear the envelope open.

Marilyn Bayard
Lilith Valentine

You are cordially invited to the Warrior Center on Thursday, August 25th at 8:00 pm. Wear comfortable clothing.

Sincerely,
Headmaster Merryweather

The summons is written in beautiful calligraphy on thick, pure white card stock. I hate every word of it. It takes all that I have in me not to throw up as I leave the invitation on Lilith's desk. It sticks out like a sore thumb among her clothes and shoes. Despite having a closet for her items, she lets them pile up on top of books and papers that we may never see again. I've never seen her study or do homework. We don't have any classes together; I wonder if hers don't assign after-class practice and essays.

Theoretically, I don't have a problem with the Warrior Center. I just thought that I'd have a little longer before I wound up there. Perhaps I might get a chance to sneak a peek at someone else mid-fight, or I'd hear about what was expected of me. I wouldn't be the first person going in with no knowledge or understanding of what I'm about to face.

The dinner bell tolls and three sharp chimes echo off the buildings. I look at the watch on my wrist and realize that I spent more time with Professor Estes than I thought. It is six pm and the sun looks like it's about to start fading from the sky. Just as quickly as I entered my room, I leave, carrying the weight of the world on my shoulders.

The hallways are empty this evening. Either students are already at the dining hall or they're holed up in their rooms. The first week has ended and so has the busy work our professors assigned us during those first few days. Now we're enveloped in studies, trying to prove to a handful of teachers that we aren't worthless. The next three months will determine what classes we take for the rest of our time at Blackwood. By Christmas, I'll know exactly what my focus will be. Assuming I live that long. I'm not convinced I'll survive the rest of the year. Between all the people who hate me, the Headmaster that no doubt wants me out of here, and the Blackwood Five, it'll be a miracle if I make it to New Year's Eve.

I wonder if we get to know our opponents for the Warrior Center ahead of time. I haven't asked Lilith much about it. For a few days at least, I thought it was all one big joke. Nobody ever spoke about the fights, not even the professors. But I guess they'd have to be speaking to me to tell me what to expect.

"Well, well, well, look who we have here." His voice triggers the fight-or-flight instincts in me. I don't even have to look up to know that I've run straight into Vale.

But I do look up. I could run away, but I'm too tired. My body says to fight even though I am substantially unprepared. "Considering this place is full of magic and magical beings, you'd think someone would have figured out a way to take out the trash."

Vale looks stunned for a second before he starts

laughing. But the anger in his chuckle makes my skin crawl. "Oh, so you're funny now, huh." He takes a step toward me, his figure suddenly menacing. A few weeks ago, I thought this man was attractive. He still is, frankly, but now everything he does repulses me instead of turning me on.

I look around for backup, or at least someone watching to keep his magic in check, but the grounds are strangely empty. Of course, on the only day that I want someone around to watch my back, I have nobody. "Something like that," I respond with a sigh. "Could we do this some other time? Reschedule for tomorrow, perhaps?"

His brow furrows with delight. There are ten feet between us, but Vale prefers to be close enough that he can breathe his hot, disgusting breath on me. "Why? You got a hot date tonight?"

His tone is teasing but in a tormenting kind of way. He doesn't say it like a friend would say it to a friend, he says it like he wants me to take a stab at my heart and twist the knife. "Yeah. I'm taking up with another demon. You know I can't get enough of you hot-headed types."

Vale's hand is around my neck before I finish my sentence and I know immediately that his muscles aren't just for show. The strength behind his fingertips pressed to my trachea tells me that I'm seconds away from being strangled to death. "God, you're such a cunt," he says with a glare. "You were a good lay for a filthy slut willing to do it in an alley, but that's *all* you were good for. I can't wait until Christiana and Eden get their hands on you."

I don't recognize the names. I reach up to grab his wrist, wrapping both of my hands around it while trying to pry myself away from him, but his grip only gets tighter.

"You think I don't know who you're facing in the Center?" He asks with a snort. "Who do you think talked Zephyrus into speaking to the Headmaster? Your roommate has garbage magic, except for the whole shifter thing. You're even worse off. Honestly, they could just send in Eden and the two of you will be chopped liver in under a minute. How does that sound? A delicious, chopped, Marilyn and Lilith sandwich."

My blood boils. I don't know if it's the lack of oxygen or anger bubbling to the surface, but one second I feel lightheaded and the next Vale is jumping back with a roar. Red marks crisscross his arms, shooting up to his biceps. I reach up to claw at my throat, coughing as I'm finally able to breathe again.

"What the fuck is wrong with you?" Vale screams. He looks from me to his arms erratically.

I look up and see his eyes flickering. The deep blue shade is muddled with red, the sign of a demon about to change. "Don't you *ever* put your hands on me again," I choke out. I wouldn't be surprised if I woke up tomorrow morning with a bruise shaped like his hand around my throat.

Vale's voice dips a couple of octaves and his skin starts to change colors. A brilliant shade of red comes to the surface, making it hard to see the marks I just left on him. "You silly little girl. You think a little fire will hurt me?"

Fire? Is that why he jumped back like he was being scalded? "I don't—" I start to say, but he cuts me off with a roar.

"I'll do whatever I damn well please." His demon form is revealed. Gone is the angry, gorgeous man who hates me. Standing before me is a hulking beast, his muscles even burlier in demonic form, rippling with intensity. "You pathetic little bitch. You think that you can tell *me* what to do?" Flames lick his skin; he looks like a walking torch.

I pull myself to my feet, determined to stand my ground in what looks like my final moments. If he kills me, at least this will all be over. I won't have to succeed in classes I'm not meant for anymore. I won't have to pretend I don't hear people calling me stupid and weak in the hallways. I won't have to worry about my roommate threatening to kill me in the middle of the night because some other burst of magic popped out of me like a damn jack-in-the-box. The afterlife might actually be quite nice compared to academy life.

"Do your worst." I can hear the exhaustion ringing in my tone clear as day.

"No!" Across the campus, I hear someone yelling and a flash of purple steals our attention. Lilith is racing across the grounds toward us, her gold gaze focused on Vale. "Don't hurt her!" She yells. "Don't hurt the baby!"

In action movies, there always seems to be a moment when the hero looks like they're about to be defeated. Someone shoots at them or a wall comes crumbling down, certain to bury the hero beneath a thousand pounds of brick and debris. The music swells to a climax, all motion slows to a crawl, and you watch as a light turns on in the hero's head. They think of some way to get out of their situation and save themselves.

It's the same for me. Everything stops as confusion ripples across my features. I notice Vale's form start to change. The flames disappear and he becomes himself again. His dark blue eyes bore into me when he flashes a look back in my direction. "What?" He asks sharply. "What baby?"

The light that turns on in my head isn't an answer to my problems though; it doesn't save me from the situation I'm in. The light that turns on is a revelation.

The explosions of power. The strange occurrences of magic. They're not from me at all.

MARILYN

Dinner is long forgotten in the wake of the news. "I-I have to sit down." Though Vale and Lilith approach, one looking confused and the other looking concerned, I can't look at either of them. The world feels like it's spinning. Is it actually spinning? I know we travel around the sun, but can everyone else see the buildings start to turn like they're on a Merry-Go-Round?

"Marilyn," Lilith crouches down, "Marilyn, are you okay?"

She sounds like she's seven leagues under the sea. Dark spots cloud my vision. "I need to lie down," I mumble to myself. Right there on the front lawn, I fall backward. The grass prickles my arms, making me itchy, but the cool touch of its blades is soothing. "That's better."

Vale hovers above me with a glare etched into his features. "Are you pregnant?" The question sounds more like a demand as if my being pregnant will somehow change how he acts toward me.

Lilith swats him away. "Leave her alone. She didn't know."

No, no, she did not. As the 'she' in this equation, the only thing I knew was that everybody hated me and I couldn't control my magic anymore. I was certain that it was a response to all the stimuli I was facing at the academy and eventually it would stop. "That was a silly thought," I giggle to myself.

"Great, pregnant and crazy," Vale announces as he crosses his arms over his chest.

I don't see the look that Lilith flashes Vale, but I bet it's a good one. He pulls out of my view and grumbles to himself about bitchy women telling him what to do.

Lilith places the back of her hand on my forehead to check for a fever. "Listen, I was in the library a few minutes ago looking for an explanation for what's been happening."

"Wait," Vale interrupts immediately, "what's been happening?"

She withdraws her hand with an impatient sigh. "God, you're annoying." Lilith makes herself comfortable on the ground beside me, crossing her legs under her and keeping two fingers pressed to my wrist to monitor my pulse. "Marilyn's been manifesting new powers, but she had no idea where they were coming from. It was like she was unaware of what she was doing."

I *was* unaware. I add commentary in my head. I try to open my mouth to respond, but my response is soundless.

"I found a book in some ancient language about crossbreeding. In retrospect, I guess I could have checked out the crossbreeding section," she muses. "I couldn't read a lick of that book. Though I didn't know she'd crossbred until I saw the pictures."

Vale huffs with even more impatience than before. "Get to the point, will you? I don't have all damn day. Some of us want to go to dinner and hang out with people we actually like."

Not me. I'd be happy to lay here for the rest of the night. When the sun sets in an hour or two, it'll be nice and cool out here. With my body feeling like it's on fire, I relish the natural AC.

Lilith keeps talking. "Well, I think she's pregnant. The magic she's been manifesting isn't hers. Or maybe it is. Crossbred babies are really close to their mothers. It seems like whatever *its* powers are, it's using Marilyn as a vessel. Or, I don't know," she adds, "maybe she's usurping the kid's magic."

I can hear Vale's footsteps on the grass; it sounds

like he's pacing back and forth. "So you're telling me that this little witch not only got herself knocked up by some other race, but she's harnessing her baby's powers? God, witches are a strange breed."

Knocked up by some other race? The only people I've slept with in a window that would facilitate this pregnancy were those damned demons. It isn't like I've been spreading my legs for half the academy.

Lilith either knows this or assumes it. She hits Vale with a glare and asks him who he thinks the father is.

"I don't know." Vale throws his hands up in the air. "I don't know what she does in her spare time. Maybe she's fucking werewolves in the forest or some shit."

Anger drives me to a sitting position. My arms itch like crazy from the grass. "Excuse you," I scoff, "I think if anyone *knocked me up*, it was you and your little posse of demented demons. I haven't slept with anyone else since the five of you drugged me and fucked me senseless." Funny how in the heat of the moment I forget that I liked the five of them fucking me senseless.

Vale's jaw drops open and he stops pacing. For the first time since I've met him, he's speechless. He looks like he's about to say something, but then he snaps his mouth closed and turns hard on his heel. I watch as he retreats for the dining hall. "Good riddance," I yell after him. "Stupid demons ruining my life."

Lilith is kind enough to let me rant for a minute without interrupting. Her hand comes back up to my forehead and she nods her head approvingly. "You're cooler now," she says with a smile, "I was concerned for a moment there. Not that I'm a doctor," she frowns.

I bat her hand away as I pull my feet under me, mimicking her position. "I can't be pregnant, Lilith. I don't know what you read in the library or looked at, but I'm not pregnant." I know she's concerned about the explosions of magic, but they aren't related to a baby. I'm certain of that. For starters, I'm on birth control.

But it dawns on me almost immediately that my parents were on birth control, too. In fact, they'd even cast a charm to prevent pregnancy, but here I sit. I relied on a little pill chemically designed specifically for my body by the doctors in Meira'mor. Could it be that it failed? And if so, I need to write a strongly worded letter to my doctor.

"Sure," Lilith agrees after a few moments, skepticism ringing in her tone, "there's a chance that you aren't pregnant. But Marilyn, how do you explain the power you've been exhibiting? We can develop new magic at the academy under the right circumstances, but yours has appeared out of nowhere. How do you explain that?"

I'm counting the weeks. Four weeks ago I was on Earth's side of the portal. Would I have been ovulating? I guess I did have my period a couple of weeks before that, but I'd need to look at my planner to be sure. I write it down each month even though it always happens at roughly the same time of the month.

"Hello?" Lilith waves her hand in front of my face. "Are you listening to me? You're always off in your own little world."

I shush her. "I'm counting," I say with a shake of my head. If I had my period two weeks before I went through the portal, then for all intents and purposes, I'm six weeks along. "When do women start showing signs of pregnancy?" At twenty years old, neither Lilith nor I know the answer to that. She shrugs her shoulders and I'm left wondering if last week's display of erratic magic was my own or the baby's inside of me. "Why would a baby use magic anyway?" I ask out loud with a nervous chuckle.

But I already know. Lilith said that crossbred babies are really close to their mothers. It was protecting me. In every situation, it was making me more comfortable. On the nights that I was hot, it made the room cooler. When Lilith was snoring, it realized that I needed silence to sleep. On the days students made fun of me, it pushed them away.

I place a hand over my belly trying to see if I feel any different. My stomach is no bigger than it was yesterday or last week. I can't feel some alien force inside of me kicking around. Maybe Lilith doesn't know what she's talking about. Maybe I'm trying to justify everything with a convenient answer. But having a half-witch, half-demon baby isn't convenient. "I definitely used protection." I am not my mother. I am not a woman who accidentally got knocked up and doesn't want to be a mom. "Well, it was a pill," I add uncertainly. "It isn't like the pill didn't work. It's supposed to prevent these types of things."

Lilith starts to play with the blades of grass beneath her, unable to meet my eyes. "I don't know. Who's to say they work between witches and demons? Did you guys use a condom? Pull out? Cast a spell? Anything besides relying on that one little pill?"

I throw myself back down on the ground, hitting the grass with a thud. "Oh, god, Lilith, I can't be pregnant because I was stupid enough to think a single pill would solve everything."

She sighs heavily and lays down beside me. I feel the brush of her arm against mine and it's strangely soothing in this chaotic moment. "It figures that my roommate would be the one to have sex with a bunch of demons and bring back a forbidden practice. The Headmaster is *not* going to be happy about this."

"Speaking of the Headmaster," I groan, "we've been summoned to the Warrior Center later this week."

Lilith takes a deep breath and I see her shaking her head out of the corner of my eye. "Of course, we've been summoned to the Warrior Center."

She's right. When it rains, it pours. And right now, we're getting drenched.

ARES

When I saw Vale across the lawn squaring off with Marilyn, I moved into the shadows. It seemed easier to watch the fight without having to back Vale up. I know that the silver-haired girl is someone we're supposed to hate, but I don't have a problem with her. She likely doesn't belong at Blackwood, but I'm not going to be the one who sends her packing her bags.

I jump from shadow to shadow across the lawn, I even stand in Vale's shadow for a moment. The cruelness of his words and actions send me running for a tree. There is peace in the shadows of the inanimate. In Vale's shadow, there is only coldness.

I don't expect Marilyn's roommate to come running up with a confession. I don't expect to see Vale's face fall as he hears the words. I stand in the darkness with my own jaw dropped in similar shock even after Vale walks away.

Marilyn and Lilith talk to each other for a few more moments. I sneak closer, disappearing into Lilith's shadow. She is warm and comforting, a soothing change of pace from the cold and dark shadows that follow most of the students.

I almost answer when Marilyn asks when women start to show signs of being pregnant. Just a couple of years ago, when my brother and I came to Blackwood, my mother and father missed having a kid in the house. By Christmas break, we returned home to find her carrying our little brother. Slade didn't care, but I was intrigued. I asked her about the process and what happens to a woman's body; she was happy to share all that she knew.

As Marilyn announces that she relied solely on a little pill, I flashback to the night in the club. Vale and Nicodemus came inside her. I remember because I knelt before her in a dingy bathroom and licked her clean. I tasted my buddies' juices and kept on licking anyway. Then I did exactly what they did, following my brother as we poured ourselves into her womb. We thought she was a human. We thought any sperm that made a race for her eggs would burn up before implanting. It turns out we were wrong.

I swiftly leave the scene, lily-padding through the shadows until I'm far enough away from them that they won't notice me. One last look at Marilyn leaves me angry at myself and the men. What have we done? How could we have fucked up so badly?

I head to the dining hall to look for the guys, but they're nowhere to be found. When I see Zephyrus' spot among the staff table empty, I assume that he must be with them. I head to the dorms to search, but once again I'm met with nothing. Where could they be? This campus isn't very large.

One last ditch effort shows me the answer. Checking Latham Hall is my last resort, but that's where they are. Zephyrus' door is closed, but a light shines through the window. I peek inside and see the other guys sitting around. Slade is on a desk, kicking his legs back and forth morosely. Vale is leaning up against a wall, his arms crossed angrily over his chest. Nicodemus is sitting, his feet propped up on a desk—always looking for comfort, that one. Zephyrus sits behind his desk with his hands steepled before him, an intense look of concentration on his face.

I startle them with a soft knock before twisting the handle and letting myself in. "Hey," I greet softly, "we need to talk."

Zephyrus gestures for me to close the door behind me. "Vale has something to tell you."

Before he can impart the news upon me, I hold my hand up and tell them that I already know. "I was watching," I admit with a wince. "I didn't want to interrupt."

Vale's shoulders tense up. He's probably thinking that I didn't help him and that was a betrayal. I should have let him give me the news and acted like I was surprised. "Anything happen after I left?" He grumbles after a few moments of silence.

I shrug my shoulders and try to find a spot close to Slade; I always feel safer when I'm around my twin. "Not really. They talked about pregnancy for a few more minutes while Marilyn tried to determine if it all added up. I think she believes it now." I know I do.

My brother sighs heavily, drawing attention toward him. "Guys, I have to admit something." Oh, god. Not again. I can't handle any more truths today. "When I said that I saw she was having what seemed like two dreams, I should have picked up on it. A halo of energy always follows her around in one of them. The other dream has always just been colors and voices. I never really understood it, but I'd seen it before."

Zephyrus asks him where and my stomach sinks as I figure it out before Slade says it. During all of those weeks we spent at home with our parents, I thought he didn't care that mom was pregnant. "My mom, a couple of years ago," he answers out loud what I'm thinking in my head. "She was pregnant with our little brother. Sometimes he dreamt, sometimes he didn't.

But her dreams never had a halo of energy following her around. So I figured that it couldn't be the same."

The joke's on us, it is the same thing. "Why do you think the little halo thing follows her?" Zephyrus asks.

Slade shrugs his shoulders and kicks his legs a little harder. "I don't know, frankly. Dream science is difficult to understand." His only passion is understanding how to better utilize his gift. He reads extensively trying to get a grasp on dreams and nightmares. Magical research, human research, foreign research, it doesn't matter. If it has to do with the subconscious mind while sleeping, Slade will read it.

"It could have something to do with the fact that she crossbred." Vale doesn't tear his eyes off the ground as he mumbles this announcement. "She didn't reproduce with a wizard."

My brother jots this information down. "I'll have to look into crossbreeding and its effects on the psyche."

"The roommate said crossbred babies are close to their mothers. Maybe it's like, following her around to protect her." We're the worst scientists in the world to be discussing this. We know nothing about women, witches, or babies. We're theorizing into the dark, hoping that we trip on the answer.

Zephyrus gets up from his seat and asks a question that only Vale and I know the answer to. The fear in his voice adds a hitch to his words. "Do we know who she reproduced with then?"

Vale makes eye contact with me. For a second, he looks vulnerable. He's always been the most capable of all of us, but right now he looks scared. So I tell them what they all want to hear. "She says she hasn't slept with anyone since the five of us."

Silence wafts through the room as I drop the bomb. Zephyrus and Slade start nodding their heads as they break down what this means. But Nicodemus is quick to ask aloud what none of us want to admit just yet. "So whose baby is it?" The question forwards every pair of eyes in the room to him. "It has to be one of us, right? How do we find out?" He pauses and grows a little more introspective. "What if we never find out?"

His questions are met with even more silence. Nobody quite knows how to respond to that. We're all in our twenties. None of us imagined having a child this young.

I look toward Vale and see his chest rise and fall dramatically. He's taking deep breaths to calm himself as he thinks through everything that's happened in the last hour. He avoids my gaze, letting his arms drop to his sides before pushing off the wall. "I need to think," he says after a few moments.

With the silence effectively broken, Slade is quick

to follow suit. "Yeah, same." He hops off the desk, nearly bumping into Vale as he flees from the room.

Realizing that he's brought up a question that even he doesn't know the answer to, Nicodemus slowly takes his feet off the desk. "I'm going to go to dinner," he says as he clears his throat. "Some food will do me good." When he leaves the room, only Zephyrus and I are left.

"You gonna go?" He asks after a minute. We all need to think about this and consider what it means, even the smartest person among us.

I guess I don't have to come up with an excuse. I just nod my head and thumb at the door. "Want me to close that behind me?"

He closes his eyes and nods. "Oh, yeah. I'll lock it behind you." I watch as his fingers come up to press against his forehead. The stress he must be feeling, the anxiety we're all feeling, is palpable.

I head out with a commiserate purse of my lips. "Sorry, Zeph," I apologize as I start to pull the door closed behind me. I see his mouth move, but I never hear his response. I'm already thinking about what the next few weeks will look like.

What the hell have we gotten ourselves into? And what do we do next?

ZEPHYRUS

I had the perfect family growing up. I was the youngest of five kids and we were all treated the same. With two older brothers and two older sisters, I thought that nobody's childhood was better than mine.

Mom took us everywhere. We visited every corner of Meira'mor from the playgrounds to the museums. She gave us access to every musical instrument she could get her hands on. She was a gifted musician, the kind that could hear a song once and play it perfectly a few moments later. Sometimes I would hear my grandparents whisper in the corners about her affinity for music. They never appreciated what she could do with a guitar or a violin, they only complained that she didn't spend enough time studying magic during her years at Ridgeview Academy. But it didn't matter to me that my mother's greatest gifts were raising kids and having perfect pitch. Between my siblings and I, we could do anything that she needed.

I remember my father being a jovial man. He had a belly like Santa Claus and the graying hair to go with it. Every winter, he took the family hunting. It was a week-long camping trip to the other side of the portal where he taught all five of us how to be ethical hunters. "If the worlds ever go to hell, I want you all to be able to provide for yourselves without magic."

Those were the days. We'd bathe in creeks and lakes, whooping and hollering all day long as we tried to stave off frostbite. The humans had the Boy Scouts, we had our dad. He showed us how to make a fire and keep it going. He taught us how to identify edible berries, leaves, and bugs. He trained us to know how to find our way home if we ever got lost. He gave us all the tools we needed to survive off the land.

My childhood was perfect. I dreamt of growing up and recreating the same practices in my own home one day. But it didn't quite pan out like that.

Instead of making it into Ridgeview like my mom or Brookhaven like my dad, The Council saw fit to send me to the Blackwood Academy. My parents didn't cast me off when they heard the news, but as the only Storm who didn't become a legacy, they were concerned. I think they searched for the darkness in me for weeks. There was something inside of me that made me fit for the school of dark magic. What could it be? That question plagued them every moment of every day.

It drove a wedge between the family and me. I grew introspective, trying to figure out what it was that could have me trolling the halls of a school traditionally meant for magical beings with dark souls. They tried to include me in the family traditions, but I sunk so deep into a depression that I couldn't pull myself out of it for holidays or birthdays.

While I was at Blackwood, I lost magic. Nobody ever talks about that. Some days it feels like the guys have forgotten what I could once do. When I walked through the doors of the academy, I was trying to master the art of levitation. I was told that if I did it right, I could learn how to fly. But fate is a cruel mistress.

I showed an aptitude for alchemy during my first few weeks at Blackwood. The other students laughed at me and said that if I loved science so much, I should head to the other side of the portal. But it wasn't that simple. I took to alchemy the way Vale took to aggression as a first line of defense. I could create and transform in my sleep. And the longer I studied the lost art of alchemy, the less interested I became in learning how to manage my levitation.

That was where it all went downhill. I stopped wanting to have a family; my studies were more important. My professor told me that with abilities like mine, I could change the world. "You have to let go of the things that weigh you down though," he warned. He wanted me to leave behind the worries of my family. He wanted me to let go of the relationships that took up space in my head. He wanted me to stop hanging out with my friends and focus my time solely on our work together. I was happy to do the first two, but when it came to my friends, I couldn't let them go. I needed something more than an enclosed lab and all the materials in the world I could wish for. Hanging out with Nicodemus, Vale, and the twins kept me sane.

I don't know when things changed, when life became about more than creation. I graduated and spent some time touring the vast lands of Meira'mor and what lay beyond the portal. I visited the labs of well-known alchemists and tried to study at their feet. But being away from the people I cared about eventually made me feel lonely. I returned with the hope that I'd find a job I loved, reconnect with my family, and re-engage the friendships I'd left behind.

I didn't think any further than that. It didn't occur to me that getting back together with my Blackwood friends meant doing some of the same things we'd done before. I felt wise beyond my years until the five of us got together. Then our time was spent together on the other side of the portal or picking on people we didn't like. Somehow, that seemed natural, so I didn't question it.

Hindsight is 20/20. If I'd have thought to ask myself, "Is this something we should be doing?" Then perhaps we wouldn't be in this situation. Marilyn wouldn't be carrying a bastard, crossbred baby that belonged to one of us. I wouldn't be lying on my office floor contemplating what this means for my future.

It's bad enough that we had sex with a witch and didn't use protection. It's unfortunate luck that she wound up getting pregnant. But it crosses a line when you think about what we are to one another. I am Marilyn's professor, at least for now. She doesn't have an aptitude for alchemy and I'll probably excuse her from my class roster soon enough. But the power dynamic still exists. We might all be adults, but there's still a firm academy rule about professors dating their students.

Will the Headmaster fire me or will I get a slap on the wrist? The academy's lab receives a great deal of funding for the research that I do. Is he a risk-averse man? Is he willing to accept the queries and questions that might come from keeping a professor on staff that knocked up a student?

But also, am I ready to face what this all means? I gave up wanting to be like my parents five years ago. I thought that love might be in the cards for me one day, but a family was off the table. I wouldn't have the time to give them the attention they deserved. So why have kids at all?

I kick myself for only realizing this now. I should have always been using protection, whether I was on this side of the portal or not. Being on Earth shouldn't have excused me from wearing a condom. What if I'd gotten a disease? Or what if I crossbred with a human? The statistics of it happening are incredibly low, but not impossible.

If my mom were here, she'd chastise me for even having to consider this. I can hear her now; I can practically see her shaking her head in shame. "There's no *thinking about this,* Zeph. You have to do the right thing. Be there for her, protect her, and bring my grandbaby home as often as you can."

My father would be angry. He dreamt of more for his life than five kids, but he loved us with all his heart. He never let us see that a horde of demon babies meant that he couldn't fulfill his dreams. In my ear, I can hear him yelling. "Man up, Zephyrus. I didn't raise you to be a deadbeat dad. This might not have been what you thought your future would look like, but it's what it is now. Get your shit together and start preparing to be a father. Being a dad is tough, but I raised you to handle it."

Their words are the motivation I need to pull myself off the floor. My back hurts from lying on the marble, but it's the kind of pain that centers a person.

Yes, this is going to be hard. It will test every fiber of my being. I'll have to face the wrath of the Headmaster and The Council and maybe they'll fire me. But when it's all said and done, who's to say this won't have a happy ending?

Marilyn is a beautiful woman. And those few minutes I spent in her hotel were practically life-changing. So why am I letting the fact that she's a witch come between us? Because Vale said he didn't like her? It's time for me to step up and do the right thing.

I head for the door, intent on marching to Marilyn's dorm and telling her that she's the one for me. I'll step up and I'll be the father her baby needs. I will become the man she wants. I'll do anything for her.

Until it occurs to me that I might not be the father and I might not be the only one who wants to step up.

What happens if one or more of the other guys want to be a part of this baby's life? Do we ask her to find out who the father is? Or can I accept never knowing if the baby in her womb is mine?

Being a father is on my to-do list. I just thought I'd be in my thirties before it happened. And it'd be with someone that I loved.

Marilyn is okay. I don't know her well, but I don't think any of us do. It isn't like we've sat down with her and discussed her theories on magic, life, and the pursuit of happiness. She was meant to be a one-night stand on the other side of the portal. We were supposed to fuck her and never see her again. She wasn't supposed to show up at the Blackwood Academy carrying a child.

If I'm being honest, I don't think this turns out well for any of us. When the Headmaster finds out she's pregnant—and eventually, he *is* going to find out—there will be hell to pay for all of us.

Merryweather has never liked the Blackwood Five,

with the exception of Zephyrus. Zephyrus showed a unique ability that Merryweather could harness for his own sadistic pleasure. The rest of us were thorns in his side that he would have gotten rid of if he could.

He's hated me since the day I rifled through his dreams and found his greatest fear. I spent weeks fucking with him, turning the sweet, virginal woman in his dreams into a literal killing machine. She chased him around forests at my behest, a loaded gun in her pocket and a taunt on her lips. "When I find you, Clarence Merryweather, I'm not going to kill you. I'm just going to hurt you a little bit."

I suppose it's my fault he went on trial for murder. One day while he walking down the street, he saw the woman from his dreams coming out of a shop. He followed her for weeks, or at least that's what came out in the trial. Merryweather denied the claim that he stalked her, saying that he'd never seen that woman before in his life. He also denied that on a night when he was in his werewolf form, he showed up at her house and ripped her to shreds.

He got off with a slap on the wrist. He even got to keep his prestigious job at Blackwood. But everyone will attest that after what happened with the woman, he turned colder, more evil. He was already steeped in darkness, but Merryweather went off the deep end after his trial.

He didn't know it was my fault until he returned to

the school a few weeks later. I was young and dumb, a fresh twenty-year-old who just wanted to press my luck with the big bad wolf on campus. I asked him if his dreams had gotten any better now that the figure-head who tried to kill him every night was dead. It took him less than a day to dig into my files and see what I was capable of.

Merryweather threatened me in the dining hall with everyone around. Students were eating at their various tables and professors lined the halls on elevated platforms. He pulled me from my seat with a genial smile on his face and asked to talk. With an arm wrapped around my shoulder, he whispered in my ear. "If you ever mess around in my dreams again, you'll be the next person I'm on trial for killing. Do you under-stand me?"

I'd be lying if I said a chill didn't run down my spine. At twenty years old, I still felt like a baby. "I understand quite clearly, sir," I mumbled the words with all the confidence I could muster, which wasn't much when faced with a man a foot taller than me.

He clapped his hand on my shoulder and gave a fake, deep belly laugh that echoed through the hall. "That's a good little demon," Merryweather chuckled. "Don't ever think you can pull one over on me. I will ruin your fucking life, Bloodstone."

I'll be the first one he suspends when he finds out

about Marilyn. He might not like Ares, Nicodemus, or Vale, but he'll get rid of me in a heartbeat.

It could be worth it though. I'm in my third year at Blackwood and as much as I enjoy the classes and the camaraderie with my friends, I haven't learned anything in these halls that I couldn't have read from a book. The library has quite a selection on the topic of dream magic, manipulation, and materialization, but half the books are out of date. I think if I were expelled from the academy, I'd have plenty of time to do all the research I wanted. I could even take a few classes across the portal and worm my way into a job studying the science of dreaming.

But if I did that, I'd leave Marilyn behind. The possibility that she's carrying my baby is the only thing that keeps me from marching to Merryweather's office right now and telling him to expel me. I just want to get this over with, but honor anchors me in place.

We all did something wrong that night. Nicodemus controlled the way she responded to us, enhancing her sexual interest for our selfish purposes. Vale was the first to come inside of her, leading the way for the rest of us to think that it was okay. Ares and I were filthy and depraved, taking her in the bathroom because we couldn't wait any longer. Zephyrus took her back to a hotel and had sex with her even after she passed out. None of us are innocent.

None of us know who the father of the baby is, either. I could handle it if it was Ares. He's my twin; we share a bond that can never be broken. From womb to tomb, we always say. But do I want to take the rap if it turns out this baby belongs to Nico? Or worse, Vale?

I want to be a father one day, but I think the way I want to raise a child will clash with Vale's parenting style. I love the guy as a friend, but if we tried to co-parent, we'd kill one another. I want my son or daughter to grow up differently than I did. There was nothing wrong with my parents or my childhood, I just want him or her to grow beyond their magic. I want them to know that there's a whole world out there full of possibilities and choices.

I've spent so many years cooped up within myself trying to figure out how to utilize my magic that I haven't experienced all that the world has to offer. I don't want that for my kid. I don't want that for anyone.

It occurs to me that Marilyn might not be able to figure out who the father is. Crossbred babies are different than purebred ones. Their magic is chaotic and hard to control, it's one of the reasons they were banned from Meira'mor a century ago. The Council found that they couldn't protect the magic world from children with erratic powers. A couple of decades later, a law was put into effect that the parents of crossbred babies going forward would be forced to terminate the pregnancy or spend the rest of their lives in prison. It was the only way they could enforce the ban on inter-racial children that threatened our universe. People were breeding in darkness, building an army of unde-featable kids and The Council had to do whatever it took to stop the madness.

The thought of Marilyn being forced to terminate her pregnancy makes me angry. This was an accident. Should she be punished for an accident? Should the rest of us be punished for that accident? Would they punish us all? So many unanswered questions, so little time.

Vale's parents have high positions within the Meira'mor government. Zephyrus' father is a minor judge. Nicodemus' mom works for the mayor of one of the largest townships. Surely they can't force us all behind bars for a mistake. There would be hell to pay as our parents came forward one after the other to defend us.

But maybe that's our answer. Instead of one of us stepping up to claim parentage of the child, maybe we all need to step up. There's strength in numbers.

I head back to McCabe Village with a plan. Maybe I don't want to raise a baby with Vale. Maybe the baby isn't even mine. But if we're all going to avoid the consequences, the answer is simple.

We all have to take the blame for what happened.

NICODEMUS

It's a common fact of life that you will grow up, get married, and have children. These values are instilled in you at a very young age. But what happens when you want to deviate from the path?

The day I turned sixteen, my mother cupped my face and cried. "You're growing up so fast, Nico," she said through tears. "One day soon you're going to start dating. You're going to find a nice girl and settle down. Then you can give me grandbabies."

I was only sixteen. She and my father had spent years repeating the process of reproduction over and over again until I had a litter of siblings. My youngest sister was only three years old and I couldn't tell if the two of them were done procreating or if they still had a few more years of childbearing to go.

I'd lived through my fair share of sleepless nights

because one of my brothers or sisters stayed awake crying. I'd seen my mom break down when the stress of parenting became too much. Maybe one day I'd change my mind, but at least at the tender age of sixteen, I didn't want to have kids when I got older. It seemed like a mantle I didn't want to bear.

For starters, I don't have any skills to pass down to a child. My father might have taught me how to cook, but those skills are long gone. When mom watched all of the kids, the kitchen duties were left to dad and me. He showed me how to roast a chicken, make scrambled eggs, and bake the perfect cake. We spent hours in the kitchen with one another, experimenting with recipes and making subtle changes that nobody ever appreciated because they didn't have a sensitive palette. When I began at Blackwood, I wasn't around much anymore. I stopped cooking because we had chefs who did it for us. Summers back home became less of a bonding experience between my dad and me as I found my interests ran more toward women than being in the kitchen. I'm sure I could still roast a chicken if I needed to, but I don't think it'd come out quite the way it was supposed to.

Cooking is a useful skill, but not when your knowledge is half-baked. I'm going to be able to teach my kid how to salt their pasta water but what about the important things? Like handling bullies or developing a sense of right and wrong? I never had to do those things. I *was* the bully. And frankly, I don't think I ever learned how to separate doing the right thing from the wrong thing. I just did what made me happy and more often than not, it hurt someone else. How does a guy like that become a good parent?

I told the guys I needed to get some food, but heading to the dining hall now sounds like the least appealing option. The thought of eating sours my stomach, so I walk in another direction. The faint scent of savory chicken is replaced with florals wafting in from the garden. Subconsciously, I allow my feet to take me there.

How many times have I slept with someone? I can't count the number of partners I've had on my hands. I've brought at least four women to these gardens alone, one for each of my previous years at Blackwood. I'm a ladies' man. And sometimes, under the cloak of darkness, a gentleman's man. I've had my fair share of partners across the spectrum of gender, dabbling in a little bit of everything. If it made me feel good, I wanted more of it.

How does someone like me change their ways and become a father? How am I supposed to give up everything I believe in to take care of a baby I never meant to have?

A bench sits beneath the glow of the moon and I walk over to take a seat. I've never felt lonely at Blackwood before. When I first started, Zephyrus was a couple of years ahead of me. He took me under his wing and taught me everything I needed to know. He showed me the secret spots on campus where you could get away with kissing a girl or throwing a punch. He taught me which professors would bite my head off if I popped off in their class. He instructed me on how to talk to the Headmaster if I ever got caught doing something I wasn't supposed to. Zephyrus is a father figure.

I'm just...me.

I go around messing with people's emotions and feelings for no reason at all. I use my magic to benefit me, including heightening a woman's lust until she's falling over at my feet. I make people feel bad because it gives me a giggle. I'm not a good person. I'm not meant to be a dad.

The cool evening breeze rustles the leaves on the ground; fall is starting to settle in. The trees are changing colors and stripping off their clothes in preparation for a long hibernation. In spring, they'll be reborn. Their beauty will return, along with their leaves, and once again they'll be clothed in splendor and dignity.

Also in spring, Marilyn will be ready to pop. I can do the math like anyone else. Nine months from the day we met is sometime in April. As the flowers are beginning to blossom again and the sun is staying in the sky longer, she'll be preparing to have a child.

There's a chance that it won't be mine. Maybe she'll give birth to an angry little demon baby that can move people around like chess pieces. I could write the kid off as Vale's and let him deal with it. I'll only be a few weeks away from graduation and I'll need to focus on my boards.

Except... what if it isn't Vale's baby? What if there is some kind of cruel, twisted God up there that thought it would be funny to have me follow in my parent's footsteps? They'd be proud of me for starting a family so young. Twenty-five is the perfect age for children in their minds. I'm young enough to keep up with the perils of a newborn but old enough to get a job and support my family.

Lavender tickles my nostrils and unlocks a core memory. It was a million years ago, it feels like. My mom set my baby brother in my arms and asked me to watch him while she went to the grocery store. I was thirteen years old and my stomach tightened like a fist. But in the hour that she was gone, he never woke up once. I sat on the couch holding him in my arms, preparing for him to start screaming, but I was met with silence. And, as I'm reminded, the sweet scent of his head.

I never quite noticed it with my other siblings, but mom never really made me hold them if I didn't want to. With Malachi, I had no choice. I pressed my nose to his forehead and breathed in deeply. He smelled warm and sweet, like bread fresh from the oven. I was hooked after that. In the months that followed, I would pick him up and sniff his little head whenever I got the chance. It was an odd thing to do as a teenager, but I couldn't explain what it made me feel.

Now, all these years later, I'm reminded of that scent. I remember mom coming home from the hospital with Malachi in her arms. He was wrapped in a white and blue baby blanket. Whenever he opened his eyes, they were the darkest shade of blue. When he was angry, his forehead scrunched up and you could see him start to shift. His skin turned a scaly red and though he didn't know what he was doing, his body changed. He was a tiny little demon baby that couldn't control his actions. And when he slept, he was a perfect little angel.

I've never wanted a child. They're loud and noisy, and if my siblings are any indication, smelly. But what if my own kid is different?

There's a 1 in 5 chance that the baby in Marilyn's womb is mine. If I wait until it's born to find out if I'm the father, how am I going to feel about missing all those months I could have made memories with Marilyn?

Adversely, there's an 80% chance the baby isn't mine. If I step up now how am I going to feel when it turns out the kid is Slade's or Zeph's?

Maybe there isn't a right answer. Maybe I just need to figure out the right answer for me.

My father never failed to do right by my mom. When she was overwhelmed with the kids, he took us away for the week to give her a much-needed break. When she needed help at bath time, he took half the kids to another bathroom and got them ready. He took us to school some days; he picked us up on others. He made dinner. He helped out around the house. He was a father. He stepped up to the plate and knocked it out of the park.

I don't have to ask myself what he would do because I know that regardless of the outcome, he'd do right by my mother. Whether the baby was his or his best friend's, he'd be there.

Being a good man can be difficult, but he's always told me that it's worth it. "Being a parent means being paid in laughter and memories," he said to me once with a wink, "it might not sound like much, but it's enough to carry me through the rest of my life."

I've been called a lot of names in my life. Bad guy. Demon. Manipulator. Playboy. Heartbreaker. I've heard it all, except for daddy. Maybe that's a new title for me to try on. And if I wear it for a while and it turns out I'm not the father after all, well, that's okay, too. One of my closest friends will be a dad and he's going to need all the support he can get.

ARES

The shadows are a cold place to live. Warmth lies in a woman.

Eden Hightower is my warmth. I met her last year during her first days at the Blackwood Academy. She was a sweet little bear shifter with an anger problem. I watched her lash out at her roommate once, tearing her nails through Christiana's flesh until she looked like a rag doll. Christiana healed herself and told Eden to do it again. I didn't realize for a long time that the two of them did this often, that it was a coping mechanism for them both. I just saw a vicious young woman whose inner beast spoke to mine.

I wasn't the kind of guy who tore into people, but I wanted to be. Vale was always the one of us that took charge. He was the kind of guy that lashed out at other people. I stood in the back and waited until they walked away, then I drifted into their shadows and listened to their conversations. Eden and Vale were the aggressive types; I was just passive.

But it was her aggression that called to me. I walked up to her one day and asked her on a date. I remember her pretty little face looking up at me as she brought her hand to my cheek and patted it hard. "You're going to have to do better than that, honey." She lit a fire inside of me.

With all that's transgressed since then, Eden still isn't my girlfriend, she's just a woman that I sleep with. I sneak her into my room in the village and hold her tight for as long as she'll let me. Some days she shows up with a singular goal: getting off. I explore her depths until she's slapping a hand over her mouth to keep from bothering Slade. Then she leaves without a goodbye. I have buried my cold body in hers for almost a year. And yet, nothing has ever made me feel quite as warm as the thought of having a child.

I am not in love with Eden Hightower, as much as I wish I was. We are habits to one another—hard, unbreakable habits. But a baby is just the thing I need to quit.

When everyone scurries from Zephyrus' class-room, shooting off in different directions, I linger in the halls. While the four of them are probably thinking about how to get out of their duties as a parent and how to pin it on someone else, I'm considering what kind of father I'll be.

I want this baby. I think it'll give me what I've spent my life longing for. I've spent my years in other people's shadows, but this baby will bring me into the light. And as dark as The Council thinks my heart is, I am more than that.

When I leave Latham Hall, it isn't to think about whether or not I want to be a father, it's to consider what the rest of my life will look like. With Marilyn by my side, I think I could spend less time drowning in other people's shadows. She's feisty and warm, a departure from my coldhearted Eden. Marilyn carries my baby in her belly, a feat Eden would rather die than do. I could fall for Marilyn Bayard; I know I can. I can make myself love her if it means having everything I've ever wanted.

Sure, I should think about the possibility that the baby isn't mine, but the truth is that I don't know if the other guys would step up to be the father this child needs. It is part witch, part demon, and it will be frowned upon by society. I know what that's like; I know how it feels. I can show it how to overcome. I'm only in my third year at Blackwood, but I can learn how to balance my classes and raise a baby.

"Watch it," someone slams into me from behind, pushing me out of the doorway of Latham Hall. I'm jostled from my thoughts and brought back to reality.

The moon is rising and there are four other demons on the school grounds right now considering what it would be like to be a father.

Vale is probably hating every second of it. He doesn't like Marilyn; I can't imagine he'd be accepting that he could be the father of her baby. He's somewhere out here throwing stuff around or lighting it on fire. He's got a temper and he probably isn't controlling it well after what we just found out.

Zephyrus would make a good father. He's kind and patient and he's always been someone I could confide in when things were rocky between Slade and me. But he's a teacher and she's a student. It's the kind of relationship that would lose him his job. If Zeph steps up to be the father, he can kiss his entire life goodbye.

Nicodemus doesn't have a paternal bone in his body. He'll probably be the first one to say that he wants no part of this. He'll slowly back out of the room until he's gone, leaving us to figure out who has to be the guy who steps up to bat.

Slade might be my twin, but I doubt that he's thinking the same thing as I am. He lives in a dream world where he spends his time conjuring up nightmares and bringing people's fears to life. I don't think he'd have to give that up for a kid, but he would think he'd need to reform himself for the good of his child. And would he even be able to do that? His magic is dark and swollen with vengeance. Could a man like that be a father even if he wanted to?

I know the answer; it's as clear as day. I step up and become the dad that the baby needs. In turn, it gives me what I need: warmth. I won't hide in its shadows the way I have with so many other people. I will dedicate my life to nurturing it and making sure that it grows up better than I did. He or she will know love and patience, kindness and joy, and lightness in abundance. They will be so well taken care of that even if they develop the same kind of magic I have, they won't feel the need to live in the shadows.

I need to end things with Eden. As much enjoyment and warmth as I've found in her, our time together is drawing to a close. We no longer want the same things. I only hope that she doesn't tear my face off the way she has Christiana's; I can't self-heal.

There's a bathhouse on the outskirts of Meira'mor filled with all kinds of creatures. The men, women, and folks in between provide an array of services to their paying customers. The darkness that haunts those halls would scar people if they knew what went on there.

I met my first witch in the bathhouse. I showed up on a dark and cloudy night in search of something I couldn't put my finger on. A connection, a roll on the hay, I wasn't sure. I asked the keeper for a witchy little thing that was flexible and didn't mind a little rough wooing. He sent me to Isabella.

I remember her dark brown, almond-shaped eyes and the way her eyelashes fluttered in the breeze, so impossibly long that I swore she couldn't see. I remember her lithe body and waif appearance, as if she didn't get food to fill in the holes carved out by starvation. I was certain that she would break like a twig beneath me.

"Do you like demons, little girl?" I asked. She couldn't have been more than twenty years old, but that was fine because so was I.

Isabella's tongue slowly slipped out of her mouth and caressed her bottom lip. She was slow to speak and I didn't know if it was intentional or because she wasn't all there. "I've never been with a demon before," she admitted in a small voice.

I shifted before her eyes. Gone was my human form and in its wake was a snarling demonic creature. Skin a dark maroon, eyes a fire engine red. The clothes I'd worn were torn to shreds, hanging off my figure like scraps. My cock throbbed as I approached her. "I'm going to tear you in two, little girl."

I penetrated her with my ribbed member and watched her open up before my very eyes. Her jaw dropped and her long eyelashes brushed her cheeks as she disappeared into the fantasy. I felt her nails on my wrists as I thrust inside of her. I watched her sweet, porcelain-like features contort into pleasure as I fucked her. I kept waiting for her to scream at me to stop. I wanted to push her to her breaking point and then watch her cry as I kept pounding my monster cock into her over and over again. But she creamed all over me instead, marking me with her lust.

A little part of me changed that day. I'd grown up in a racist household with parents who often put down other species within Meira'mor. I remember their words; I hear them rattle around my brain often.

The succubi are fine, but their magic is silly. They're angry little girls with the power to control a man's lust. Never stick your dick in one because you're likely to wind up pulling back a nub.

The shifters think they're scary, but their greatest power is another form. Many of them have self-healing magic; give them a reason to use it.

The werewolves consider themselves the bullies on the playground, but nobody out bullies a demon. The key to handling a bad dog is to tie it up and give it a few kicks until it behaves.

The witches hardly belong in Meira'mor; they're glorified magicians. Herbalists and potion masters? More like scientists with a need to prove themselves. They're second-class citizens to the rest of us.

I went to school with different races. I learned math beside a dragon shifter that could barely read. I was taught the basic principles of science with a succubus lab partner. I made out with werewolves under the bleachers during gym class. But I stayed away from the witches until my night at the bathhouse.

I expected Isabella to crumble beneath me. I chose her because I wanted her to feel humiliated; I wanted her to cry out in pain because of what I was doing to her. I wanted her to feel like the second-class citizen my parents told me that she was.

Except none of those things happened. The only screaming I heard was Isabella's cries of pleasure. She wasn't embarrassed when, out of frustration, I flipped her onto her belly and fucked her from behind like a dog. I watched her long, slender fingernails dig into the blankets as she shoved her ass back begging for more.

I left the bathhouse feeling unhinged. Why couldn't I make her feel my hatred and anger? Why was she immune to it?

I never had to deal with witches at Blackwood Academy. There was no one there that I could back into a corner and demand answers from. I had to take my queries back to Isabella on nights when I knew no one would notice my absence. When half the school was cheering on their favorite team in the Warrior Center, I was asking Isabella questions that I didn't dare approach my parents with.

"I don't feel like a second-class citizen, but many people treat me like one," she admitted over a mug of tea and spices. "The same was true when I walked the streets in a business suit working for the Meira'mor government. Witches and wizards helped build

Meira'mor, and yet we're treated like we don't belong. Many of us have ancient blood in our veins, but it's the shifters who rule over us, it's the demons who think they know better. Without the witches, you would still exist, but your existence would be limited to the shadows beyond the portal. *We're* the ones who thought to create a home for the magical."

I didn't remember any of that the day I found out what Marilyn was. I reverted back to my racist, preexisting notions. Witches were dirty. Witches didn't have real magic. Witches couldn't compete with us. It was jarring to think those words while simultaneously dreaming about Marilyn. In my dreams, I tried to humiliate her the same way I'd tried to humiliate Isabella. But it always ended up with the two of us making love. I always seemed to wind up lying beside her in a bed or beneath the beams of the sun on a warm spring day.

My dreams were jarring, to say the least. And every night as they drifted from one scene to another, it made me angrier. I'd grown up hating witches for no other reason than my parents said that's what I was supposed to do. Knowing that I'd gone to the human's side of the portal to find solace in the depths of a non-magical creature and realizing I'd had the best fuck of my life with a witch tested my anger like no other.

My parents would never understand if I showed up

with a pregnant witch. They wouldn't welcome me with open arms and accept Marilyn for who she was. They would ask if I'd gone crazy and consider having me checked out by a physician.

There's no way that I can be a father to her baby. I can only hope that the 80% chance it isn't mine wins out. Zephyrus would be a great dad; I hope he's the father. He wouldn't have to explain to his parents what happened and bear the shame that comes with it. His parents are nice; they'd try to support him.

But if the baby is mine, if Marilyn is walking around with my little demon in her belly, I need to prepare. The Headmaster is likely to expel her and turn her over to The Council. The baby's life will be threatened and so will our freedom. She'll have to choose between saving the life of her child and spending the rest of her days in prison, or having the baby's life terminated.

I've seen what that baby can do. I've been burned by its touch. Whatever is inside of Marilyn has powers that the rest of us could only dream of. And if it came from my loins, I want to be there to watch it grow up.

Is this what it's like to be a parent? To think one minute that you can't do this and think the next that it's the only thing you want?

My feet move me toward McCabe Village and I'm not the only one. Maybe it's a coincidence that Ares is headed this way. After all, it's where we all live. But there's a glint in his eye that makes me pick up my pace. I can tell from the way he moves that he's going to Marilyn's. Is he making a declaration for the baby, too?

MARILYN

"My parents already hate me, you know. I'm going to get expelled and they're going to kick me out and then I'll be homeless, pregnant, and carrying an illegal baby." I'm lying across the smallest part of my bed with my feet leaned up against the wall and my head hanging off the edge. All the blood is rushing to my head. "An illegal baby that could be one of five guys. Do you know how that sounds? I don't know who my baby daddy is. I'm a damned cliche, Lilith."

Lilith sits in front of her desk with her feet kicked up on her pile of clothes. She wears a bored look while she thumbs through the pages of a book. "Oh no," she says in a droll tone, "you got to have great sex with five dudes. I feel so bad for you."

From this position, she's upside down, but no

matter how you slice it, she doesn't look interested. "Lilith, this is bad. I'm going to be kicked out of school when the Headmaster finds out."

"Depending on who they give me as a replacement roommate, that could help me in the Center. Do you think you could speed up the expulsion so someone gets assigned to me before Thursday?" Lilith keeps flipping through pages.

"I don't even think you're reading that," I accuse, suddenly feeling frustrated that she isn't paying attention to me. I haven't complained about being bullied or harassed since I started here. I kept my problems to myself for the most part. All I want is a few minutes of sympathy before I get off my ass and start thinking of a solution.

Lilith slams the book closed and chucks it on her desk. In a few days' time, it'll disappear beneath another wave of clothes. "It's a stats book from previous years' Warrior Center fights if you must know, and I've read it a dozen times already. I'm trying to prepare for our fight because pregnant or not, we're still going into that pit and facing off against a pair of individuals who are probably a lot stronger than us. So forgive me for not attending your pity party when I'm throwing my own over here. My mom will likely attend and watching me get my ass kicked isn't how I thought my first Warrior Center battle would end."

Am I an asshole? Because it feels like I might be an

asshole. I've spent the last couple of hours thinking about myself and my problems. And while they affect some of Lilith's life, she still has her own shit to deal with.

I remember coming home after school some days and complaining about what a hard day I'd had. My dad would always sigh with annoyance and tell me that my problems were fleeting and I shouldn't worry about them. Then he'd go off on a tangent about how he had a case to deal with that would get a fifteen-year-old stripped of their magic and that was much more important.

But the thing was, I knew my problems were small in the grand scheme of things. What I needed was his reassurance that even though what happened today would be forgotten by next week, he still cared. His problems were more serious, but that didn't make mine any smaller.

I've been minimizing Lilith's concerns for the last few hours because I thought mine were the only ones that mattered. I was doing to her what my father had done to me.

The realization hits me like a Mack truck and I instantly feel bad. "Is there anything I can do to help?" I offer with a wince. "You're a dragon shifter, right? You can shift and breathe fire and knock people around. I can repel and attract things," I add with a wan smile. "That could be useful, right?"

Lilith crosses her arms and keeps her eyes trained forward. "Maybe. Depends on what you attract and repel. But you said we're facing off against a bear shifter?"

I nod my head the best I can in this upside-down position. "That's what I remember Vale saying." Just mentioning his name causes a wave of anger to wash over me. I'm thrown back into my emotions for a split second.

"I'm not very large in my shifted form. I'm growing, but not fast enough." Lilith brings her perfectly manicured hand up to her mouth and starts chewing on the nails. "I'm probably two, maybe three sizes larger than a bear. That isn't much depending on what her roommate can do."

I can't remember the names that Vale told me, otherwise I'd share them with Lilith and let her scope out our competition. "Is it really going to be that serious?"

She nods her head absent-mindedly. "There are a bunch of smaller fights that will occur over the next few weeks. Once October hits, Merryweather will have an idea of who should go up against who. In the larger battles, people have been seriously injured. Those fights are always people with destructive magic, which means we probably won't be invited to participate, but we'll still have to prove ourselves in the meantime."

My hand comes up to my belly as if to protect the

tiny child inside. "I'll do what I can, Lilith. I promise. I don't want to be the reason either of us gets hurt."

Before she can respond, there's a knock on our bedroom door followed by a scuffling of feet and the sound of voices in the hallway. Lilith looks at me and raises an eyebrow. "Think it's your little demon horde coming to cut the baby out of your belly?"

A shiver runs down my spine. "I sure hope not."

"It's open," Lilith announces loudly. "Maybe they'll spice up our evening. It hasn't been chaotic enough."

The door opens and I'm met with Vale and Ares trying to fight their way into the room. "Get out of my way, Vale. I want to talk to her first."

Vale wraps an arm around Ares' neck and holds him back. "You're being ridiculous. You don't know what you want."

Lilith and I look at each other and try to stifle a laugh. As they make their way inside, step by scuffled step, Zephyrus comes up behind them. "What the hell," he mumbles, "what's going on?"

"Beats me," Lilith announces as she gets to her feet. "But if you guys don't stop soon, I'm going to call security."

Ares and Vale stop long enough to frown at her. "What security?" Vale asks, confused.

She points toward me. "The little demon love child

in Marilyn's belly. You should see what happens when it perceives that she's in danger."

Vale unwraps his arm from around Ares' neck and straightens up. Ares starts smoothing out his shirt and clearing his throat. "Listen, we didn't mean—" he starts to say.

"Christ on a cracker," someone says from behind them. Every head turns toward the door as we see pretty, charming Nicodemus stroll through. "It's a party in here and no one invited me?"

"You made it, didn't you," Vale groans.

Frankly, I'm fascinated by the change of pace. I've gone from moping about my circumstances to being the life of the party. "Does someone want to explain why they're here?" That was the wrong question because everybody starts talking all at once. Even Lilith adds her two cents to the conversation and starts yelling that they're all a bunch of idiots, but I think she's being facetious.

When they start getting louder and yelling over one another, I feel my fingertips start to tingle. This has happened nearly every time magic has exploded out of me and if we're attributing this to the baby, I bet we're seconds away from another accident. "Guys," I try to talk over them, waving my hands in the air to get their attention, "guys! Shut up!"

This ceases the yelling, but not by choice. I see their mouths open and close but no words come out.

"Great," I mumble, "I've done it again." Or the baby has, I guess. It was too loud, so it silenced everything around me. "You've really got to teach me that trick," I tell the fetus with a hand positioned over my stomach.

"What the," a voice breaks through the quiet and I see Slade striding into the room. "Uh, what's happening here?" He looks at his friends attempting to talk. Vale is pointing his finger angrily at me and Zephyrus is standing with his arms crossed over his chest and a sour look on his face.

It's probably time that I get up and survey the damage. Or at least try to convince the tadpole in my womb to straighten things out. "Sometimes when he senses danger, he solves the problem," I tell Slade as I attempt to roll over and climb off the bed. "This happened to Lilith once when she was snoring and she got really upset. Maybe I should leave them like this. Though honestly, I don't have any control over it." If I could harness this baby's magic, all of our problems would be solved.

Slade nods his head slowly in agreement. "Right," he says. "Well, I guess if they can't speak, I'll tell you what I came here for. When you tell the Headmaster that you're pregnant or whenever he finds out or whatever you plan to do, I think we should all take responsibility. They can't expel us all. And Vale's parents will fight tooth and nail before they let their only child wind up behind bars."

The idea has merit, though I think the Headmaster would be more than willing to kick me out of Blackwood without so much as a goodbye. He might keep the Blackwood Five, but not the witch who defied all the odds and wound up at his school. "Yeah, but isn't he going to want to know who the father is?"

The mouths of our company slowly stop moving as all eyes turn toward us. "Probably," Slade winces, "but I don't know if paternity tests work the same on cross-bred babies in the womb. So, while there's a chance you can find out who the father is, there's a higher chance that you won't find out until after it's born. Since I doubt that the Headmaster is willing to wait until then before taking action, I suggest we all claim paternity and refuse to back down."

With the blood rushing back into my body from lying upside down, I suddenly feel a little woozy. Or maybe I'm just a little surprised by this sudden declaration that all of these men are willing to put their lives on the line for me. "Wait," I frown at him. "What about the actual paternity? Does, do, well," I struggle to find the right words to say, sputtering out phrases that make no sense. "It's nice that you want to help everybody from getting expelled or thrown in prison, but what about what comes next? Ultimately, someone has to parent this child. I'm twenty years old and I don't have a good role model as to what a parent is supposed to be. I'm just supposed to fight for this baby's life and then what?"

"We parent together." Zephyrus' voice breaks through the magic. A sincere look appears on his face as he takes a step away from the pack. "I don't know about you guys," he looks back at the other demons, "but we've done everything together for years now. We're best friends. Even when we butt heads, we're the people we turn to when we need help."

The spell must be broken because Nicodemus adds to what Zephyrus was saying. "My mom was over-whelmed by kids, she probably still is. Even with my dad around, it was a full-time job raising us. If we stick together, it could help everyone. Parenting is hard and I'm sure that none of us know what it takes."

Ares looks to his brother and I watch as the two of them exchange a deep look. Slade solemnly nods his head yes. "We wouldn't mind doing that," Ares announces. "We really do share everything. I mean, that's why we're here." He has the grace to look abashed by the comment.

Vale is the wild card. He looks around at the other men with his brow knitted tight in concentration. Nobody knows what he's thinking and for a second, I think he's about to blow up. His jaw tightens and his fists clench at his waist. "You guys have stood by me through thick and thin. I've done things that I'll never admit to anyone but you. If you want to do this together, I won't say no."

Lilith claps her hands together and breaks the tension. "Wow. Beautiful. I love this for all of you. Now, Vale, Marilyn said you knew who we were going up against in the Warrior Center. Mind sharing that information so I can do some research? If we're going to protect your little spawn of Satan, I'd like to know what to prepare for."

It's the perfect segue. While they discuss amongst themselves who we'll have to face, I take a moment for myself to process what just happened. I went from having five possible baby daddies to having five men decide to step up to bat to keep us out of prison. Hours before, they all hated me, and now they're talking about the best way to keep me safe.

The blood rushing from my head has had plenty of time to trickle back into my extremities, but I still feel lightheaded. "I need to sit down," I mumble to myself. None of them hear me; they're hanging on Ares' every word as he tells them what Eden is capable of.

I'm going to be the mother of an illegal, crossbred baby. And the men who knocked me up are putting aside their differences to come to my side.

Did I cross the portal by accident? Am I in an alternative universe? Because that's the only thing that could explain how a witch and five demons are coexisting and co-parenting.

MARILYN

It almost feels like this is what was supposed to happen all along.

After the men finally left on Monday night and I regained control of my sanity, I fell into a blissful sleep. I watched as my dreams unfolded and showed me what life could be like. With a white picket fence and a light blue house as the backdrop, I watched the five demons become daddies.

Vale acted like an overprotective father to the baby girl running around with silver eyes and long, dark hair. He warned her about Slade and Ares, who kept taking her on questionably safe adventures. Zephyrus sat on the front porch and read to her as nighttime started to fall on the field. He answered all of her questions: Why is the sky blue? Why do we exist? Why does she have five daddies? Zephyrus patiently explained it all. Nicodemus taught her how to protect herself and her heart from boys. It was a strange feeling to wake up and realize the idyllic house in the country was just a figment of my imagination.

The next morning, I didn't make it more than a few feet outside my dormitory door before I ran into Nicodemus. He leaned up against the wall with a couple of cups in his hands and looked around with vague interest as the other students got up and around. "Hot chocolate?" He offered as I approached. "I'd have gotten you coffee, but I remember my mom limiting herself to one cup a day when she was pregnant. I figure maybe you can't have it or something."

I grabbed the warm cup from his hands and took a sip, savoring the explosive flavor on my tongue. "How many brothers and sisters do you have?" If these men were going to be in my life, it was important that I got to know them.

Nicodemus filled me in on his family tree as we walked to the dining hall. Halfway there, we were joined by Ares. He appeared out of nowhere and apologized immediately. "Shadow walking," he said with a mumble, as if that explained why he left his brother behind.

Slade caught up after a few long strides and I felt like the most popular girl in the school. I was being escorted to the dining hall with three unmistakably attractive men at my side. I thought their show of support was quite nice, but it didn't end there. Over the next three days, I noticed everything had changed.

Vale stopped angrily throwing me across hallways and slamming me into walls. When we passed one another on the fourth floor of Latham Hall as he left Professor Estes' room and I entered, he didn't taunt or tease me. "How are you feeling today?" He'd ask anxiously, then practically bounce on his toes as he waited for the answer. I watched his eyes drift to my belly on more than one occasion. I wasn't showing, but it didn't matter. I could see the fervor in his eyes as he watched me.

Zephyrus pulled me aside after his lesson on Tuesday. "I'm going to drop you from my class," he said with a solemn look. "For starters, this doesn't seem like something you're going to excel in." He was right. I had no gift for creation or destruction. I didn't understand the principles he shared with us and the idea of turning one thing into something else seemed foreign to me. "But even more important than that, when the Headmaster finds out about all this, I don't want to be accused of taking advantage of one of my students."

I would see him less. Zephyrus was always the nicest of the demons, but I understood what he needed. The more distance he put between us, the better the chances would be that he kept his job. "I understand. It'll free up my schedule for other practical classes anyway."

"I don't know if this will be a problem, but if some of the magic you're displaying is the baby's," he looked around quickly to make sure no one was eavesdropping, "then some of the things you exhibit this year will set you up for classes you can't complete next year. Once it's born, we don't know if you're going to lose magic or if what the baby's done through you has expanded your power."

It left me thinking about the future. As I drifted slowly to my next class, I wondered what this revelation meant. Would I have to retake my first year? Would I fail all of my second-year classes? What happened if a student stopped exhibiting the abilities that got them into certain classes? It was a question that haunted me as I listened to the history professor bore on about Wearers figuring out what the source of their magic was should they ever lose their item.

The demon pack surrounded me in between classes and during meals. Ares and Slade walked me to classes. Ares told me that he broke things off with Eden. "I didn't tell her why, just that it was no longer working for me." I still didn't know who she was. She could have sat next to me and I wouldn't have known it. Slade didn't have much to say, so he stared down everyone who looked at us. Big or small, it didn't matter, if they threw a side glance our way, he tightened his fists and let them know he was ready to fight if they were.

Nicodemus turned out to be incredibly thoughtful. Throughout the day, he'd bring me water or snacks, always with a happy smile and an eye on my stomach. "My mom loved being pregnant. She said it was the best part of raising kids."

I didn't notice much of a difference yet. The baby wasn't big enough to kick or roll around. I barely realized that it was inside of me until I performed magic I wasn't used to. I guess I had cravings, but it was more of a heightened enjoyment of roast beef at dinner or grabbing two ham sandwiches at lunch instead of one. If I didn't know there was someone inside of me controlling my reaction to what I ate, I might have written it off as being hungrier because I was working harder.

Lilith's attitude toward me never changed. She encouraged me to figure out how to harness the baby's energy for the fight on Thursday. In her spare time, she was slowly sneaking out every book about witches, pregnancy, and crossbreeding that she could find. One by one, the books showed up on my bed all throughout the day; I had enough reading to last me a lifetime. I started having to hide the textbooks under my bed in the event that someone came in and saw what I was studying.

Everything seemed different after that explosive Monday afternoon. I had a friend in Lilith. I had people who cared about me. I almost thought that everything was turning around. I was going to have my dream academy experience after all.

Then Thursday rolled around and as classes ended, Lilith snatches me away from Professor Estes and demands that we talk about the upcoming battle.

"So it looks like Christiana is about as useless as they come. She can heal, but she doesn't have any other magic. If she does, it hasn't been revealed yet because nobody I talked to had any information about her." Lilith speaks as fast as she walks. We don't seem to be headed anywhere in particular, but Lilith seems insistent that we make it there quickly. "Eden is going to be the one we have to worry about. She was an accomplished shifter before she arrived. Last year she excelled against different shifters in the Warrior Center and—"

I cut her off. "Last year? She isn't a first-year? They're putting us up against an *established* team?"

Lilith sighs impatiently and explains that this particular fight is probably rigged. "It's probably meant to humiliate us when we're torn to shreds and recovering in the infirmary. Pay attention. Eden is known for snapping bones in half for the sheer enjoyment of listening to them break. Stay away from her and let me handle it."

Dinner starts in a few minutes, but my stomach feels queasy. The pregnancy books Lilith has been urging me to read all talk about morning sickness in the first trimester, but this is the first time I've felt acutely nauseous. I'm not sure if it's because of the baby or the impending fight. But whatever it is, I decide not to eat. I have snacks in my room for later, assuming I survive.

What won't tear as easily beneath the claws of a bear? I decide on leather.

Marilyn is wearing jeans and a t-shirt. "What?" She frowns as I lead her toward the forest. "The note said to dress in something comfortable. You do not look comfortable."

My attire is motorcycle club chic. I have on a pair of black chaps and a leather vest. None of this will survive a shift, which is why I also have a bag with a change of clothes in it. But in the event that Eden takes a swipe at me before I shift, I want to be protected.

We hear a dull roar as we enter the forest. Just as I suspected, the audience is larger than normal. "These smaller fights aren't usually well-attended," I tell Marilyn, "at least in the first few weeks. People don't really care about shifters fighting shifters or werewolves fighting succubi." The unspoken truth sits between us: they're here to see what the witch can do. Does she belong here or was she incorrectly placed?

Rumors about her magic have gotten out. I've heard people talking about what they've seen her do. I like my roommate, I really do, but if they knew that half her power belonged to the result of an accidental pregnancy, they wouldn't be so curious. "Don't let the crowd distract you. Don't pander to the crowd's requests," I instruct. I feel like a mother, but someone has to take the reins. She's been focusing nonstop on the fetus in her womb but tonight she needs to put that behind her. If we aren't careful, the Headmaster might let Eden kill one of us.

Once we make it to the Warrior Center, we're met with a clearing the size of a football field. On each side are bleachers and they're both filled with raucous students already cheering for our opponents. I can't tell who is here in support of Eden and Christiana and who is here to see if Marilyn gets eaten by a bear.

Standing at our corner of the field is Marilyn's horde of men. Even Zephyrus lingers near the pack, much to the disapproving stare of Headmaster Merryweather. "We've got some support, at least," I mumble as we walk up to them.

Vale has a stern look on his face as he brings us into the fold. "They have the support of the crowd and the home-field advantage. They've done this before and they've been successful at it," he reiterates.

Marilyn is nodding her head in agreement with her eyes focused on the ground. I should have drilled her more on what to expect. It wouldn't have been fair if we went up against another pair of first years, but the Headmaster ensured a good match by pairing us against a bear with a healer that can keep her going forever.

"They've provided you with stuff that you can throw," Nicodemus tells Marilyn directly. He's right. Along the sides of the field are cinder blocks, barrels, and bricks. It isn't much, but it's enough to see what she's capable of. "But I think they're expecting the majority of the fight to be between Lilith and Eden."

I'm not afraid of her. I was when I didn't know what her roommate was capable of, but now that I know Christiana can only heal Eden, the trick is to leave her with so many cuts and bite marks that it can't all be healed at once.

Merryweather doesn't give us a lot of time to prepare. Once we're here and he sees us chatting with the Blackwood Five, he calls the field to order. I don't know who's amplifying his voice, but he can be heard halfway across campus. If there's anyone left in the dorms who might have the vaguest interest in this fight, they'll hear him and head this way. "Good evening, everyone, and welcome to the first Warrior

Center battle of the year. Today we have Marilyn Bayard and Lilith Valentine facing off against Christiana Baptiste and Eden Hightower. Marilyn is a witch and Lilith is a dragon shifter. Christiana is a succubus and Eden is a bear shifter. Tonight's fight should be interesting. May we have the fighters come to the floor."

We cross the field in what feels like slow motion. I look at our competition and try to size them up. Christiana is tall and slender with cheekbones like a model. She walks in a way that makes every eye on the field look her way. Eden is muscular for a woman of twenty-one. While many of the women here try to slim down and look like the Succubus Squad, she seems to embrace her brawny physique.

"Shake hands, everybody," the Headmaster announces with a smirk on his lips. I notice his eyes darken as he looks at Marilyn. I don't need to read minds to know that he's imagining Eden inflicting serious damage on her.

Christiana smiles prettily at us as she gently reaches out to shake our hand. Eden grips my fingers in her hand like a vice. "I've been looking forward to this all week," she says with a devilish little giggle.

To Marilyn's credit, she doesn't crack a smile or look afraid. She stares through our two opponents as though they're nothing more than windows.

"In ten seconds, the bell will ring. You'll keep

fighting until it rings again. If you can't get up, your partner has to carry on. If both of you are down, the bell will ring early. Points will be scored based on ability and performance, among other factors that the judges will take into account." Merryweather turns around when he's finished, walking away and leaving the four of us to decide how to proceed.

Marilyn and I take several steps backward, our motions mimicked by Eden and Christiana. The succubus makes her way toward the edge of the field, distancing herself from the fight as much as she can. If she is unable to perform her duties, Eden won't be able to continue rampaging over our team if she's injured. They were formidable opponents with this strategy last year and I know that they're going to be hard to beat.

When the bell rings, Eden shifts in two seconds flat. I barely realize it until I see her charging with her cavernous mouth open and spittle flying. Marilyn is the first to return fire, testing her magic by picking up a brick and repelling it in Christiana's direction. It falls short by a few feet and this causes the succubus to cackle.

Eden doesn't come for me. Her course changes by a fraction as she approaches and I can see that she's headed for Marilyn. Eden's healer is in danger and she'll do anything to keep Christiana safe.

That's enough watching for me. Before Eden

makes it to Marilyn, I shift into my dragon form. Purple scales shimmer beneath the halogen lights illuminating the field. I hear the audience react with ooh's and aah's as they look at me in my purest form. I am twice the size of Eden and I use a wing to bat her away like a fly.

Eden lands on her ass thirty feet back. She shakes her head and roars loudly enough that it shakes the entire Warrior Center, then she sets her sights on me.

I see Marilyn out of the corner of my eye. She's lifting her hands and in response, cinder blocks from the sidelines come to life. She pushes them in Christiana's direction with more power than before, but this time the succubus dodges the attacks with nimble grace. She hops from foot to foot laughing at Marilyn as she goes, shouting out taunts.

My own fight commences when Eden catches me off guard. I stared at Marilyn for too long, leaving me open to attack. The bear launches itself at my neck and I roar in pain as she digs her teeth into my leathery skin. The battle is on.

Our blood mixes together when I nip at her paw. I don't want to mangle her and I'm not the type to go for the throat, but the bite does its job. She pulls back and blindly claws at me with her uninjured paw. I spike her with my tail, a jarring blow right to the stomach that sends her flying backward. She smashes into a barrel that Marilyn helpfully repels in her direction.

The crowd is going wild. I take stock of my injuries while Eden gets to her feet and shakes off the fall. My neck is bleeding and my tail feels bruised from slamming into Eden. But this isn't as bad as it could be, nor as bad as I thought it would be.

Marilyn is really getting into the fight. I see her maneuvering multiple items at once, each sent in the direction of Eden's healer. Christiana has her hands up high wearing a gold band that looks similar to Marilyn's; she must be a Wearer as well. She channels her magic toward Eden while dodging Marilyn's attacks. In no time at all, the bear is back on her feet as if nothing ever happened.

That's how it proceeds for several minutes. I take a hit and then Eden does. I bleed a little, Eden bleeds a lot. Christiana heals Eden's wounds and Marilyn tries to distract her. My partner manages to get one good hit in, but it's with a brick. Christiana is momentarily off her game when the item comes flying into her stomach and she sinks to her feet. But by the time Eden and I take a few more swipes at one another, she's back up.

The moment it all changes is when Eden gets in a deep cut across my neck. We've been parlaying shots back and forth this entire time, but she digs her nails in a little deeper as she swipes across my throat. I am rocked backward with pain and a strangled howl escapes from my mouth. The audience starts to scream and cheer as Eden approaches Marilyn. With me out of the way, she has unfettered access to the witch.

Marilyn's primary focus is Christiana and for a few seconds, she doesn't even notice Eden stalking closer to her. But as the crowd's roar becomes louder and people are screaming Eden's name, Marilyn turns her attention to the salivating bear only thirty feet away.

I get to my feet to help her, but the blood loss makes me woozy. I stumble on my back two feet and I'm forced to all fours to keep my balance. I'm in a prime position to breathe fire on Eden, but I don't have to.

I see fear in Marilyn's eyes for a split second, she shudders as Eden starts to close the gap between them, then the magic happens.

Not unlike her first day of classes, Marilyn produces some kind of force field that knocks Eden backward. Except this time there's a distinct barrier between Marilyn and everyone else. An iridescent half-globe surrounds her, jutting out by ten feet on all sides. There was once a look of concentration on her face, but it has been replaced with shock.

I look to the Headmaster to see if he's going to do anything, but all I see is glee in his eyes. He's letting the students scream his wishes. As they yell for Eden to get to her feet and tear Marilyn apart, his delight only grows.

Woozy or not, I have to shake off the fog I'm under due to blood loss. If Headmaster Merryweather isn't going to end this fight, I have to get back in the game. I can't quit.

In the stands, I see my mother sitting with the other professors. She has a look of determination on her face that revitalizes me.

We will not succumb to these girls; we will not accept defeat.

MARILYN

God bless this baby. I don't say that enough. With Eden bearing down on me, it comes to my rescue faster than Lilith does. When barrels bounce off the bear like they're nothing, the baby is what saves me.

I don't know why I'm holding my hands up; the force field magic isn't mine. But the second I let them drop by my side, it disappears. The translucent semi-circle shatters and I'm met with a strange silence from the crowd. They were once cheering Eden and Christiana on, but now they stare at me with hotly debated confusion.

I open my mouth to apologize, but the words stick to the back of my throat. *I'm sorry, Eden. I didn't mean to do that. I thought that I was in danger and it was the only way I could protect myself.* If she could read my mind, this would be easier.

The crowd resumes screaming at Eden, telling her to get to her feet and finish me off. I watch as the bear shakes her head and narrows her gaze on me. Behind the big brown eyes of her shifted form, I see anger. I can tell that if given the chance, she will rip out my entrails and eat them for dinner.

"Oh, boy," I mumble to myself and look around. Where's the Headmaster to call the fight? Shouldn't he do something about the way she's staring at me like I'm a piece of jerky? But Merryweather looks pleased with himself. On the sidelines, he stands with arms crossed over his chest and a Cheshire Cat grin on his lips. He would rather watch me die than intervene.

Lilith is raring back to her full height, eyes directed at Eden as she opens her mouth to rain fire down on the bear. I watch her enamored, wishing that I could perform anything at her level of competence. She is a beautiful, hideous sight as she breathes fire from her lips, leaving scorched Earth on the battlefield.

My distraction is my downfall. In the horror and delight of watching Lilith's performance, Eden attacks as she evades my fire-breathing dragon roommate. I'm thrown to the ground and the wind is knocked out of my lungs. I can barely hear the din of the crowd above Eden's roar. She unhinges her jaw and thick, foul-smelling spittle flies at my face.

I'm sure that the fight only lasts for a few seconds, but it feels like an eternity. Eden raises one of her massive paws and swipes it across my chest. Her nails dig deep into my skin, ripping shreds into my body. For a fleeting moment, I think about what a nice life I've had.

A dad who cared more about the bottle than me. A mom who was never around. A world that hated me for what I was.

Okay, maybe my life hasn't been *that* nice, but it's mine. I thought I'd live to see a ripe old age, complete with a husband and maybe a couple of kids if we got around to it. I didn't really have plans for my career, but I thought the academy would help me decide what I wanted to do.

Just a few days ago my mother said that I was being ridiculous when I thought that Blackwood might kill me. I only hope that I'll live long enough to tell her 'I told you so'.

The pressure of Eden's body lifts after what feels like an eternity. I lie staring up at the night sky unable to move. Warm blood drips down my chest, tickling my skin as it pools beneath me. The crowd is still screaming, but they sound so far away.

"Don't worry," I feel a set of hands slip beneath me. I open my eyes and Nicodemus is hovering above me. "I've got you."

I don't remember closing my eyes. What

happened? I open my mouth to ask, but the question dies on my lips. Nicodemus picks me up and starts jogging across the field. I close my eyes again, the brightness of the halogen bulbs hurting my head.

"Merryweather is calling for the fight to be finished." A voice joins us after what feels like only a few seconds later, but when I venture to look around, I find that we're in the forest with the lights from the Warrior Center disappearing behind us.

I'm blacking out, I think to myself.

Nicodemus mumbles something under his breath that sounds suspiciously like *'fuck the Headmaster'* but I can't be sure. "She's losing a lot of blood," he adds louder, "I'm not taking her back."

I want to tell him that's good, I don't want to go back. I'm freezing and my head is pounding. I feel like I'm having the worst hangover of my life.

I close my eyes one last time to escape the passing of trees overhead; the sight is making me dizzy. I am jostled around in Nicodemus' grasp, but that's okay. I trust him to take care of me. I don't know why, it just feels like he'll keep me safe. The memory of the last three days rocks me to sleep.

I don't know how long I'm gone this time. It could be five minutes or five hours. I wake to the smell of antiseptic and raised voices. Someone hovers over me with their hands moving over my body. I'm hooked up to an IV that pumps some sort of fluid into my wrist.

"She's got to go." The distinct voice of Headmaster Merryweather is the first that I hear. "She doesn't respect our traditions. She doesn't belong here." Someone tries to calm him. A masculine voice that I don't recognize soothes him with a few whispered words.

"What's going on?" I manage to squeak out. My throat feels sore and my chest feels heavy, but the latter is from bandaging wrapped tightly around the wounds Eden carved into me.

The woman waving her hands over my body stops abruptly. "Thank God," she whispers. "You're awake." She's a doctor, I think. Her all-white coat is dappled with blood. Is that my blood? Or someone else's? A shudder runs down my spine. "Gentlemen," she announces loudly over the arguing, "she's back."

Back? Where did I go? I start to sit up since the bed has me lying flat on my back, but I can't move my arms. "What...?" I lift my head and look down the front of my body.

Vale is the first at my bedside and he wears a ragged look on his face. "You're secured to the bed, Marilyn," he purses his lips, "they know." With a solemn little pause and a sigh, he repeats, "They know everything."

NICODEMUS

I like to think that whatever being exists in the heavens didn't give me destructive magic because it knew I couldn't handle the sight of blood.

"Is she dead?" Zephyrus asks after Lilith launches herself into Eden, the dragon pushing the bear off of Marilyn. His face is pale white, devoid of all color except the bright red blood swirling around her.

Ares stands with his jaw on the floor. He runs a hand through his short hair and opens and closes his mouth repeatedly. Words escape him.

The arena is tinged with a little of everybody's blood and looking at it makes me feel lightheaded. Still, with the other demons standing around just watching, someone has to do something. I spring into action before I have the chance to tell my feet what to do. They move forward on their own, stepping onto the field as I quicken my stride.

"Nico!" Slade calls after me. "Merryweather didn't ring the bell." He sounds unsure as he says it, as if he knows he should be following me.

Merryweather can go to hell for all I care. Marilyn is bleeding out; I can feel it in my bones. She doesn't move as I get closer, she doesn't register the fight between the dragon and the bear, she doesn't even bat an eyelash when the Headmaster starts yelling at me to get off the field.

When I reach Marilyn's body, my stomach twists and churns with disgust. She lies in a pool of her own blood and the shirt on her chest has been ripped to shreds. Her skin is crisscrossed with cuts that look so deep they'll never heal. I get on my knees beside her and tuck my arms under her body. Marilyn's eyes flutter open and my heart almost stops out of elation. "Don't worry," I reassure her as I pick her up off the ground, "I've got you."

She doesn't say anything, she just stares at me with those curious silver eyes. The ends of her hair are tipped in blood and all I want to do is bathe her, but I race across the grass for the infirmary instead. Marilyn's eyes close as she slips away from me once more.

I'm off the field and into the tree line before one of the Blackwood Five races behind me. Vale is hot on my heels and when he catches up, he grabs Marilyn's wrist to feel her pulse. "Merryweather is calling for the fight to be finished," he says grimly.

Marilyn's eyes flutter open once more, weaker than before. "Fuck the headmaster," I mumble under my breath. I won't let him kill this woman or the child in her belly. "She's losing a lot of blood." And I tell Vale in no uncertain terms, "I'm not taking her back." To take her back would be to lose her. As it is, she closes her eyes again and slips away for the last time.

We leave a trail of her blood on the floor of the infirmary when we arrive. A nurse sits at a desk at the entrance and her jaw drops when we walk in. "Wh-what happened?" She gets to her feet and ushers us forward.

Vale grits his teeth and tells her that we came from the Warrior Center. I hear her grumble about the barbarianism of the Headmaster making students fight one another. Surely she sees the outcome of fights like this all the time. "Put her on the bed. I'm going to get help."

I'm reluctant to set her down. In my arms, she's safe. Her face has a deathlike pallor and she's cool to the touch.

"Set her down," Vale tells me gently, a hand on my shoulder. "The doctor is going to heal her. She'll be alright, Nico."

God, I hope so. I set her down on the bed and

watch as the white linens turn pink and then red. "Where are they?" I ask with an edge to my tone.

As if on cue, the doctor and nurse appear at the end of the infirmary. The nurse looks almost as pale as Marilyn does while the doctor strides across the hall determined. "We're going to need to cut the rest of these clothes off," she announces as she pulls up by Marilyn's bedside. "We need to see the extent of her injuries. Please, wait behind the curtain." A second later, the nurse pushes us back and pulls a curtain around Marilyn's bed.

"What if she's seriously hurt?" I ask Vale. "What if the you-know-what is hurt?" I'm afraid to say the word *baby* with the doctor only a few feet away.

Vale shrugs his shoulders; he's at a loss for words. We stalk around the room anxiously while listening to the doctor mumble incantations under her breath and see the nurse grabbing a variety of instruments as she enters and exits the makeshift room.

"What's happening?" Slade, Ares, and Zephyrus finally arrive, out of breath and hair askew. "Jesus, Nico," Ares looks at me, "how much of her blood are you wearing?"

I look down at my chest and realize that I'm drenched in red. In my haste to get her here, I didn't think about her bleeding all over me. My nausea over the sight of blood seems like a distant memory.

Vale answers Ares' first question. "The doctor is

taking care of her now. She'll be fine," he adds, but I can't tell if he believes it.

The doctor rips back the curtain and we all look at her. The once-white lab coat is now covered in blood. "She isn't healing. What attacked her?" Zephyrus gives a quick and succinct rundown of what happened in the Warrior Center while the doctor nods her head slowly. "None of that should prevent her wounds from healing unless the bear shifter in question had them tipped with some sort of poison."

Slade looks beyond the doctor at Marilyn. She lays there exposed, her body covered in dried blood. "Her wounds look healed. What's the problem?" He demands with an attitude.

The doctor shoots him an impatient look. "Her external wounds are healed, yes," she sneers, "but she is still crashing. We are giving her blood and trying to stabilize her, but either she's in the throes of dying regardless of what we do or there's something you aren't telling us."

"Tell her," I hang my head. "If it helps, tell her." Every eye in the room turns toward me. I know what they're thinking, that this is a mistake and we're all about to be in deep shit, but what other choice do we have? We either tell the doctor about the baby or watch Marilyn die. While it would be easier for all of us to not have to take responsibility for this, it comes at a cost none of us can bear.

Vale straightens his back and squares his shoulders. I see his jaw tick as he formulates what he's going to say. "Marilyn is pregnant," he says solemnly. "She's carrying a crossbred baby."

You would swear that we were back in the era of the Salem witch trials and we just announced we'd found a witch. The doctor crosses herself before rattling off a series of instructions to the nurse. "Call the hospital and have their neonatal team come out. Get ahold of The Council and let them know."

"Why do you have to tell The Council right now?" Zephyrus steps forward. "Can't it wait?" The nerves in his voice are evident.

The doctor shoots him a glare before returning to Marilyn's body. She holds her hands above her bloodied patient and shakes her head. "The Council has a special unit for crossbred babies, including doctors and nurses who know far more about a situation like this than me. All I can do is try to keep your friend alive until they arrive. Let's hope that's soon."

There's a sinking in the pit of my stomach. I knew we'd have to tell people eventually—Marilyn couldn't make it through nine months of pregnancy and give birth without anyone noticing—but I didn't realize it would be so soon.

"For humor's sake," the doctor sighs, "do you know what race the child's parents are?"

I make eye contact with each of the men. She isn't

asking outright who the father is, but that question will come. From the doctors or the Headmaster or The Council, or maybe all three. We need to figure out what to do when it happens, but in the meantime, I answer honestly. "She's a witch, he's a demon." She doesn't need to know any more than that.

The doctor closes her eyes and starts mumbling incantations once more in a long-forgotten offshoot of Latin. I try something similar.

God, if you're up there, let her live. It isn't much, but the words are spoken in a language I'm not familiar with: fear.

"We'll raise the bed." Someone behind me takes pity on me and elevates the head of the bed. I suddenly see a host of people in the room.

The other four demons stand behind Vale. In the corner, Lilith is being cared for by a nurse. At another bed, Eden has several doctors applying some sort of antiseptic to her burned skin. Christiana is nowhere to be found, but her appearance isn't necessary. A dozen men and women in lab coats stand around staring at me like I'm a lab experiment and not a person.

"Miss Bayard, is it true that you are carrying a crossbred baby?"

The man who asks isn't covered in blood, but he holds a clipboard and is poised to take notes. He looks like he's leading the pack as the others behind him stay silent and watch with curiosity. "Yes." Vale said they knew everything; there is no point in lying now.

The man nods his head and scribbles on the clipboard. "How far along are you?"

Though my head is thick with discomfort, I count the weeks. "Five weeks since conception, seven since my last period." All of the baby books that Lilith gave me said that pregnancy technically begins at the start of your last menstrual cycle, which makes me seven weeks along with my bouncing baby demon.

More scratches from the pen on the paper. The room is oddly quiet, even Eden stops complaining about the pain the doctors are putting her through and watches intently. "Have you experienced any discomfort?"

The questions go on in that vein for a few minutes. I answer as quickly as I can, listing off the strange occurrences of magic that started shooting out of me nearly two weeks ago. The doctors standing around us look on with disapproving stares. The door of the infirmary opens and a group of suited individuals walks through. I recognize them immediately: The Council.

"I think that's all for now," the doctor looks up from his clipboard. "You seem to be healing fine now that the CBB team has had a look at the child and brought it out of distress. We will need to monitor you and the fetus for another couple of days. At this time, due to the blood loss and shock, we aren't going to move you. You'll need to stay here and rest while we keep an eye on your vitals and ensure that nothing else goes wrong."

Headmaster Merryweather shoots the announcement down immediately with a vehement no. "Absolutely not," he insists. "I don't want her here."

The doctors look at him as if he's nothing in their eyes. After all, he is an academy Headmaster. While his position earns him a great deal of respect, his behavior negates all credibility. "Sir," the same doctor begins to talk.

"It's Headmaster," Merryweather corrects with a glare. He wears his title proudly.

"Headmaster," the doctor reiterates with a generous smile, "she will not be moved. If that is a problem, you may take it up with The Council, but we have the authority here due to the circumstances."

Merryweather looks to the entrance where the suited Council is standing. Every one of them watches with half-hearted interest and a few smile wanly while making no attempt to come to his aid. He waits for someone to speak up on his behalf, but when they don't, he turns his attention to me with a snarl. "Then I want to speak with her. I want to know how and where she did this on my campus. I want to know who the father of her child is. I want her punished to the fullest extent of the law."

The doctor once again stops him with a soothing

voice that is no less condescending than before. While he is gentle in the way that he speaks, he is firm. "While we will permit you to have a sit-down conversation with Miss Bayard, now is not the time. Her body has been put under a great deal of stress and we need to be cautious as we proceed. We do not need her or the fetus going into shock again. Do you understand?"

It's the first time I've seen the Headmaster look flustered. He looks at everyone in the room one after the other, searching for someone who will support him. But when no one takes his side, when no one backs his claim, he explodes with anger.

"You are expelled," he points an accusing finger at me. "You are a rule breaker and you do not exemplify the qualities of a Blackwood Academy student. You will gather your things and leave the second you're allowed out of this bed. Do you hear me?"

I saw this coming, but it's still a shock. I don't know how to respond and my mouth just hangs open as I search for the words.

Thankfully, Zephyrus comes to my rescue. With The Council standing off to the side waiting for their turn to speak, he helpfully throws Merryweather under the bus. "Come off it," he says with a glare, "you've been looking for a reason to expel her since the day she arrived. You never trusted The Council's decision to place her here. If she'd have failed a class you would have tried to figure out how to get her tossed out." It is the boldest I've ever seen him. He stands his ground and his voice never wavers.

The Headmaster clenches his jaw but keeps his eyes trained on Zephyrus. "It's true that I haven't taken too kindly to her presence, but I have always followed the rules," Merryweather insists. "I would not have expelled her without reason and this seems like reason enough, don't you think?"

Zephyrus opens his mouth to respond, but the Headmaster talks over him before he has the chance. "And frankly," he roars, "once I find out who the baby's father is, he is going to be expelled as well. This kind of behavior isn't acceptable at Blackwood Academy. It is repulsive and against the laws governing Meira'mor. I will not harbor a fugitive in these halls."

Slade pushes through the crowd of demons and stands by Zephyrus' side. I look at his fists down by his waist, clenched in anger. "I'm the father of her baby," he says without an ounce of hesitation, daring Merryweather to expel him on the spot.

But before the Headmaster can kick him out, too, Nicodemus steps forward and puts a supportive hand on Slade's shoulder. "I'm the father of her baby," he says with confidence.

Maybe it's the hormones or the blood loss, but I start tearing up. A week ago these men were ganging up on me as often as they could. I considered leaving the school because I felt bullied and alone. Now, one by one, they're all standing up for me.

"I'm the father of her baby," Vale says next. He wears a smirk meant to poke at the Headmaster.

Ares smiles as he walks up to the line of demons and joins them. "I'm the father of her baby."

It is just the boost of confidence that Zephyrus needs. With his career on the line, he stands up taller and raises his head high. "I'm the father of her baby."

Headmaster Merryweather looks at the five of them. Together, they are a formidable group of young men. I should know, I've slept with them and faced off against them alike.

When it looks like no one else is going to say anything, Merryweather looks back at me and lays the blame squarely on my shoulders. "You're a deceptive little witch, you know that," he glares. "I hope you're proud of yourself. You didn't just ruin your life, but you ruined the lives of five good men."

I wonder if he would think that if he'd known that none of this was my fault. Would he feel the same way if he knew that it was Nicodemus' magic that had me hopping from one demon to the next? Would it matter if he knew that none of them used protection?

"I hope The Council burns you at the stake." He growls one last time before turning on his heel and storming out of the room. We hear the infirmary door burst open and we're spellbound in silence for a few seconds before it comes crashing shut.

"Follow him," the leader of The Council comments quietly. "We'll need his testimony."

There are another few moments of quiet as everyone looks around. Something needs to happen, but nobody wants to be the person who makes the first move.

Thankfully, Lilith bats away the nurse fussing with her and gets to her feet. I can tell that she wants to say something quippy to cut the tension, but one look at The Council tells her to keep it to herself. Instead, she walks over with a semi-nostalgic look on her face. "You did great out there, Marilyn, before you almost died. I knew I'd like having you as a roommate," she says with a smile. "I knew you'd fuck shit up."

The words are spoken so quietly that only I can hear them. She reaches out to grab my hand and I squeeze hers in response. I am still secured to the bed, but it feels good to touch another person. I feel like I'm having an out-of-body experience and Lilith's touch grounds me. "You weren't so bad yourself, Lilith Valentine."

It spurs everybody to start moving, but it's exactly what I need to anchor myself to this moment. Our lives are about to change and I have no idea what that means.

Lilith and Marilyn break the spell of discomfort that the Headmaster put on us. The doctors tending to Eden's burns finish patching her up while the hustle and bustle of the room starts back up. The Council, standing quietly by the entrance, nod their heads in our direction before convening with the neonatal team. We are almost left alone.

"Excuse me," a nurse announces her presence, "but I'm going to need a vial of blood from the men."

"Why?" I glare at her. She's just doing her job and I shouldn't be upset, but I can't help myself. We're desperately teetering on the edge of expulsion and prison and every new step that a medical professional takes leads us closer to falling off. We knew that this would come, but I think we all secretly hoped it would be easier.

The nurse girds her loins against the onslaught. I see her back straighten as she makes eye contact with me. "You and your friends have admitted to possibly being the father of an interracial child. The CBB team would like to run some tests to see if they can determine who the father is."

Slade places a hand on my shoulder and the gentle squeeze of his fingers reins me in. "Vale," he says quietly like a warning.

She's just doing her job; I have to keep reminding myself of that. It is not her fault. "Fine. We'd like to speak with Marilyn first, but we'll be by to give you a vial in a few minutes." The resignation in my tone makes me cringe. This is why you shouldn't get involved with women or relationships; it always ends badly.

Thankfully, the nurse doesn't press any further. With our agreement in hand, she nods her head approvingly and walks away.

"Did you need some alone time?" Lilith tilts her head. "Because I'd like to reminiscence on all the good times my roomie and I shared before she gets carted off by the law."

Marilyn snorts as she shakes her head. "You mean the times you weren't speaking to me? Or the times that you were mad at me? Or the ones where you had to steal books from the library to support my illegal decisions?"

Lilith looks off into the distance before nodding her head. "All of them," she says with a grin.

We spread out around Marilyn's bed, each of us taking a place near her. Zephyrus and Nicodemus stand near her head on either side, followed by Ares and Slade. I am at the end of the bed taking her in little by little. Marilyn's silver locks are matted with blood. The doctors might have gotten the blood-soaked clothes off of her, but they didn't wash her hair. She looks so small in the hospital bed with her bodice bandaged and everyone standing around her.

"Things have not always been the greatest between us, but Marilyn, I think I speak for all of us when I say that we're here for you no matter what happens next." I wish I would have been the one to say it, but Zephyrus beats me to the punch. He proves once more why he deserves to be the father of this baby. He is gentle and kind and he always knows the right thing to say. All I know how to do is cause problems.

Slade clears his throat, pulling Marilyn's attention toward him. "I know I poised all of us taking the blame as a defense mechanism," he mumbles, "but I really do want to be a father. If you'll have me, of course," he adds hastily.

A lump rises in my throat. We all agreed to this days ago, but now that we're facing the consequences of our actions, the implication is somehow more meaningful.

"I know what people say about me," Slade continues, "but I'll make a great dad. I want to help you teach our baby how to live in the present, not in fantasies. I've spent so many years in darkness and this is my chance to leave the dream world for the real one."

Ares reaches across the bed to his twin, holding up his hand for Slade to grab it. It's an intimate gesture that his brother returns quickly. "You're a good guy, Slade," he says with quiet adoration, "you're going to make a great father."

When I think about all the things we've done over the years, it doesn't make a good resume. We've hurt people for the sole purpose of watching them break. We've done things that would haunt a lesser soul. Standing here today, we know that we've made mistakes that will change the course of our lives. We've been tied together since we were kids by twisted beliefs inflicted upon us by our parents and society. The pain that we've doled out always had a price, we just never had to pay it until today.

"We're all going to make good fathers." It's funny how you become nostalgic in your dark moments, but sometimes it leads to revelations. "Because Zephyrus is right: we're here for you no matter what happens next." I twist my eyes upward to the well-dressed men and women standing near the entrance. The Council watches us curiously as the doctors explain their findings. They will pass judgment on what happens next; they will determine our fate.

Marilyn looks down at her belly with hesitant tears filling her eyes. "Maybe we should terminate," she whispers, "it would be easier on all of us. The Council would respect that decision and none of us would face jail time or worse." The unspoken 'worse': having our magic stripped from us.

Nicodemus places a hand on her arm right next to Lilith's and looks at her with fierce determination. "If this baby wasn't crossbred, would you keep it?"

It's a question that haunts Marilyn. She doesn't drag her eyes away from her belly or look at any of us, she just keeps staring at her stomach. "I didn't have good parents, guys. I don't know what it means to be a mother. I don't even know if I've ever really wanted to be a mom." I see Lilith's hand squeeze Marilyn's tightly in reassurance. "But this child has protected me when I was in danger and kept me safe when I needed it. I've never had someone look out for me like that before. And I want to do the same for it. I don't know if I'll be any good at being someone's mom, but I want to try."

It's a tender moment. Everybody reaches out to touch her, even me. I can only reach her ankle, but it's enough. For one fleeting moment, we are all connected.

Then we hear a little *ahem* from behind us. Eden

stands a few feet away looking worse than I've ever seen her. She has bandages covering her burns and the tips of her hair are singed from the Warrior Center. "This is touching, really," she says in a dry tone, "but knock it off." Ares gives her a hard glare before asking her to walk away. "Why should I?" She squares her shoulders to stand up for herself. "We had the Warrior Center win in the bag. Your precious little witch should have bled out on the field. Taking care of you," she looks at Lilith, "should have been no problem. You think a few burns are going to stop me?" The hairs on her arms stand up in response. "Christiana would have kept me going long enough to finish carving my initials into your neck. You would have walked around this school with a pretty little EH scar on your throat."

"Enough," I try to stop her, but Eden is a force of nature.

She twists her attention to me and dark brown eyes take in my whole body. "You know what they're going to say about *you* when you're gone? They won't remember all the insane shit you did to other students or the reputation you once had. They're going to remember you as the weak little demon who gave it all up for an even weaker witch."

Once upon a time, words like that would have stirred me to action. I would have reared up with all the ferocity I could muster and thrown her through a window. But some things are more important than proving a point. "Enough, Eden. Nobody cares." It sounds like resignation and in a way, it is. I'm not the same man that I once was. And for the foreseeable future, I will be constantly changing. I don't need the defense mechanisms and anger management outbursts I once had.

When Eden realizes that she's not going to get a rise out of me, she turns her attention to Ares. "This is why you broke up with me, isn't it," she accuses. "You left me for a dirty little witch who fucked her way through your friend group. She's probably slept with hundreds of men. Did you even feel anything when you were inside of her?"

If The Council can hear what's happening, they say nothing. As the doctors disperse, the suits huddle together and talk amongst themselves. Everyone leaves us fighting an invisible battle based on jealousy and misplaced anger.

"We were never a couple, Eden. You used me for sex the same way I used you." He doesn't take his hand off of Marilyn's thigh as he speaks. I watch as his fingers dig into her skin a little deeper, knuckles turning a brilliant white as they swell with frustration.

"Just admit it," Eden taunts, "you're only here because your buddies are. You never could stand on your own two feet. You're just a follower, Ares Bloodstone, you always have been."

Where I keep my anger to myself for the first time

in my life, Ares lets his explode. He releases Marilyn and steps away from the bed, feet taking him to Eden's side. "And what are you? A bully? A bitch? Do you identify as either of those things?"

Eden is tall for a woman, but even she looks dwarfed standing in front of Ares. To her credit, she doesn't back down. "Proudly," she responds between gritted teeth.

"You're lucky I have something to live for." Ares' posture goes slack after a few moments as he starts to laugh.

"That little twig?" Eden looks past him to Marilyn and rolls her eyes. "I almost snapped her in two. Give the two of us five minutes alone and I guarantee she won't come out alive."

Ares stops laughing but there's still a dangerous smile on his face as he looks down at Eden. "Do yourself a favor and don't ever touch Marilyn again, don't even think about it." He tosses a glance back at us. "She's got friends now. And if the baby doesn't take you out for threatening its mother, well," Ares crosses his arms over his chest, "one of us will."

The prospect of being a father is changing us all and I've never been prouder.

MARILYN

I am on pins and needles when the door to the infirmary opens a day and a half later and the Headmaster walks in with The Council on his heels. He looks positively pleased with himself, wearing a grin that can only be described as nefarious.

For the last thirty-six hours, the Blackwood Five have barely left the hospital wing, let alone tried to find out what would happen next. Ares wakes up from the hospital bed he's been sleeping in and scrambles to his feet when he realizes who's walking our way.

Zephyrus, who has the most to lose, seems to stand the tallest. He straightens his back and wears determination and two-day-old clothes that are starting to smell. "Headmaster," he greets in a solemn tone.

Merryweather looks him up and down before turning his eyes toward me. While Lilith is nowhere to be found—she's been spending her nights sleeping in a real bed, unlike the men—the Headmaster notices the presence of my demon entourage. "Good," his lips curl up even more, "you're all here. I'd hate to have to repeat this message."

The tension in the room hasn't diminished since this whole ordeal began. I've seen moments where everyone was at peace, but none of us have forgotten that our fate hangs in the balance.

"As of this moment, the five of you are expelled from the Blackwood Academy. Marilyn Bayard, Vale Nightshade, Nicodemus Nyx, Ares Bloodstone, and Slade Bloodstone," he calls each of our names in turn. "Your things are being gathered by trusted staff members as we speak, set to be delivered to the front gates post haste.." Merryweather turns his attention to Zephyrus and the smile falters a little bit. "It is with a heavy heart that I have to say you are fired. An affair with any student would be bad enough, but an affair that led to you fathering an illegal child is unforgivable. Your things are also being collected."

Though we expected this and talked into the wee hours of the morning about what we could expect, it still hurts to hear it out loud. I've been at Blackwood for two weeks and now my time here is up. I wonder if I can attend another academy. Once the stain of our illegal activity has been removed from our names, can we go somewhere else?

"Miss Bayard, I have given you time to heal and as of this morning, the doctors report that you and your *child*," he sneers, "are no longer in any danger. With that being said, you will be summarily escorted from the campus by these fine individuals." He gestures toward The Council. "At this time, you are no longer a student of mine nor my responsibility. Gentlemen," Merryweather bows his head toward the men, "she is all yours."

If the Headmaster could, I bet he would flip us off as he walked away. But in the name of professionalism, he simply turns on his heel and leaves without looking back.

While the seven members of The Council are considered equal, one stands in front of the rest and takes charge of the situation. "Good morning, I am Nevan Gustall and I am The Council representative for racial integrity. This position covers many areas and responsibilities, but it predominantly places me in charge of interracial breeding. I have been told that you are pregnant with a demon's child, is that correct?"

His voice is buttery soft and he smiles at me as if we're talking about the nice weather outside instead of the laws that I've broken. I slowly nod my head yes. "It was an accident though," I start to tell him. "We didn't intentionally breed an interracial baby. It's actually a funny story. See, I was on the other side of the portal and —"

Nevan holds his hand up to stop me. Quite literally, the words end on the tip of my tongue. "Miss Bayard, at this time, we will not be hearing your story. There is a protocol that we must follow." He lowers his hand and I feel my tongue loosen in my mouth. "Currently, our team is looking into the paternity of your child. You insinuated that it could be any of these five men, is that correct?" I nod again, not trusting myself to speak. "Vials of blood were drawn from them, yourself, and the fetus two days ago. While our interracial neonatal team tries to procure the results, you will be placed behind bars."

Thankfully, he pauses after dropping that bomb. My heart races in my chest and my head starts to feel thick and heavy. "Prison?" I ask in a detached sort of way. "But I thought—"

Once again, Nevan stops me. "You will be sent to a minimum security facility until the paternity is determined. At that time, you will go to trial to plead your case. The Council will select a jury fit for this type of case and you will have ample time to share your stories. A verdict will be determined once you and the father have made a decision about the future of the fetus. This process should take no more than a few weeks."

A few weeks? Does that mean three weeks? A month? Two months? How long will we have to stay behind bars? "Please, you have to understand that this wasn't the intended outcome. We never meant—" I'm getting sick of this man's magic shutting me up. Every time Nevan lifts his hand to speak over me, it feels as if someone is twisting my tongue.

"The Headmaster reassured me that all of your items would be waiting at the entrance to the school. Please, gather anything that you have in the infirmary and follow me. We will need to start this process as soon as possible."

My heart sinks as I'm forced to get out of bed. While the members of The Council give us plenty of room to gather our things, they only stand a few feet away and watch us carefully. If they think I'm going to run, they're sorely mistaken. My body still feels like lead and shifting my weight from foot to foot is almost as difficult as trying to tell The Council what happened.

"Now is your chance to back out," I tell the demon horde as we fall in line. Members of The Council stand behind us and in front of us, escorting us to the exit of the infirmary. Once we're outside, we see a mountain of suitcases by the wrought iron gates in the distance. Just a few feet beyond that are two black vehicles with their engines on. "If you want to take back what you said about stepping up, I wouldn't blame you."

Vale grabs my hand as we walk across the lawn. A few students stop and stare. Fingers are pointed in our direction and the whispers begin. By the end of the day, everyone will know that we've been expelled. Will the Headmaster tell them why or will he let them tarnish our names and reputations by thinking the worst? "I'm not leaving your side, Marilyn. We started this together and we'll end it together."

Nicodemus grabs my other hand and my heart swells with pride. "What he said. I'm not afraid of spending a few days in prison. Whatever trial this is, we will make them see that our actions were innocent."

Zephyrus, Ares, and Slade line up on either side of the men. We take up the entire walkway and then some as The Council directs us to the exit. "We knew what we were signing up for when we said we'd do this together," Ares reassures me.

"We've always done everything together," Slade adds. "You're a part of us now, so you will get to know what that's like. It's quite comforting to be surrounded by people willing to experience everything with you."

A shiver races down my spine as we move closer and closer to the gate. I look at the ivory buildings that I thought were so beautiful just two weeks before. I try to take a mental snapshot in case I never return.

"Nothing will ever be the same after we walk through these gates," Zephyrus announces ominously.

Men climb out of the vehicles and start opening doors. They gather the suitcases and load them in the trunks one by one. They are solemn and disinterested in the individuals they're transporting.

I wonder if anyone told our parents what happened. Has my dad surfaced from his drunken haze to find out that his daughter has broken Meira'mor law? Has my mother crossed the portal long enough to find out that I won't burden her this Christmas with my presence? Have either of them been told that they're about to be grandparents? Would they be more excited to have a grandchild than they were to have a kid of their own?

I don't know if or when I'll find out the answers to those questions. But for now, I take a deep breath and squeeze the hands holding mine. I am an adult. I made the choices that got me here. And whether I wind up behind bars for the rest of my life or lose my child, I am the one who has to bear those consequences.

As we step through the front gates of Blackwood Academy, everything changes. I am one of the most dangerous creatures in Meira'mor and I am about to be imprisoned.

I wish I could have said goodbye to Lilith. In the end, she turned out to be a pretty good friend. I give the school one last look before I'm ushered into the car that will take me to jail. Memories that could have been tug at the strings of my heart. I wanted my parents' academy experience for so long, but it wasn't in the cards for me.

With a strange sense of calm, I climb into the vehicle and watch the sunlight and colors dim behind the privacy film. A new experience stands before me that's unlike anyone else's before. I embrace my fate with a deep breath. Sandwiched between demons, I only look forward.

The future begins now.

For bonus content, go to jesidonovan.com/ blackwoodbonus.

The next book in the series, Stoneward Asylum, follows Marilyn and her merry band of demons as they face prison and the trial.

How do you keep five demons and a witch from breaking the law?

I rolled the dice and fate turned on me. A trip to the other side of the portal changed my life forever. One accidental pregnancy and a near-death experience later, I'm in the back of a car taking me straight to Stoneward Asylum with my five baby daddies right next to me.

The prisoners don't take too kindly to new arrivals. I might only be here for a few weeks, but that's plenty of time to learn the ropes. There's a new demon squad on the playground and when they decide to challenge the Blackwood Five, all I can do is hope that we don't become chopped liver before our trial starts.

The Council is determined to serve justice, but between the baby and the prison war, I don't know which will get me first.

HAVE YOU LEFT A REVIEW?

Reviews help new readers determine if a book is right for them. I would appreciate it if you left a review or recommended Blackwood Academy on Bookbub.

I would love to know if there was something about Stoneward Asylum that you'd like to see. Email me at jesidonovan@gmail.com to discuss your expectations!